P

Poverty, Prison, Positive

Rachel I. Leonard

PAGE PUBLISHING, INC.
New York, NY

First originally published by Page Publishing, Inc. 2015

ISBN 978-1-68213-429-0 (pbk)
ISBN 978-1-68213-430-6 (digital)

Printed in the United States of America

Acknowledgements

I would like to express my gratitude to
"him whose name is above every name".
I want to thank Page Publishing;
more specifically, Diana, Kathryn, Patrick,
and the rest of the team for their patience and
diligence of helping me present my
best work to you.

To

My wonderful baby girl, Ta'-ria,
who loves to read, I love you.

1

There was conversation in the mass media that this day would come, that there would be a draft of the American people. I just didn't know that my day in the draft would be today. I had heard whispers in the neighborhood that the government was going to conduct another draft that concerned economic matters not military. In 2010, the government conducted a census in search of all the citizens who lived in poverty within our population. None of us poor folks knew at the time of the census that the data collected would be used to establish a Poverty Residential Act in 2015. The Poverty Residential Act stated all American citizens who lived below the line of poverty will be drafted into a prison called No Where for a sentence not shorter than life, with the exception of those citizens who were unemployable veterans, disabled, or retired with limited income—they would be ordered to live in the surrounding area of the prison in Freedom City, Freedom, the fifty-first state of America.

This draft caused my family and I to remain hidden in my mother's home for five years. All the time we lived with my mother, I searched for some means of employment using updated technology and the old-fashion way of knocking on doors with a paper resume hoping I could place us above the poverty line and disqualify for the draft. But that fatal day arrived, it was too late, my number was up in the lottery.

* * *

The draft and petition papers I submitted to the courts lie weightlessly on my chest, while the hard floor of carpet anchors my back to my mother's living room of her old home like a boat that's been docked. I heard a knock on the door that sounded like all the body weight of a two-hundred-pound man balled up in his fist. The constant knocking continued while my body refused to defy gravity, rise, and greet the unwanted visitor. I was anchored to the floor with immobility because moving was an unconquerable challenge to my defeated mind. I just couldn't move us into any income, with all the ideas that poured out of my large head to support five children, so why move at all? Lying here, my body feels more cold than hot as the November breeze from the old windows argues with our digital furnace about the appropriate temperature of the house. Listening to cascading water travel through the walls each time the toilet is flushed drowns the sound of our neighbors' outcries and resistance to an eviction from their homes for their crime of poverty.

My mother silently maneuvers her tall frame through the house, throwing as many of our belongings into garbage bags as that bang, bang, bang of displacement hits the door, and I lie here with no strength to help. I want to sleep. Sleepiness and exhaustion come with my brain's new roommate, multiple sclerosis. MS is a bit pushy about having the most space in such a tight area, so it spreads its legions across my brain like a blanket of stars across heaven, making it difficult for my brain to direct the traffic of information throughout my body without causing exhaustion. Sleepy in the midst of this crisis, this accusation of being a criminal against the rich, against America, from the imagination of the government, I nod off, dazed, watching my children open the door to their sealed fate of struggling. Holding the hands of my children, I crawled from the floor into a stand, and walked away from my mother's home to load a white prison bus.

As we take our seats, my conscience submerging into the DVD of my mind pushing pause, play, stop, and rewind of the trial in refutation of this draft I heard my attorney, Grace, who defended me against a prosecutor named Supercilious, contest the draft on the basis of my educational status, bachelor's degree, versus my income status of unemployment, trying to convince the court that a higher education excluded me from this draft and prison. Supercilious refused to drop the charges of poverty based on education alone. She rebutted that I was drafted because I was unemployed, sick, and with children, thereby I was contributing to the debt of America, which is now against the law in the year of 2020.

My thoughts of the trial were interrupted by the sound of the stopping bus at a gas station in Illinois, I could hear the driver inform the inmates that we were to take a fifteen-minute break before picking up more inmates in Hardin. He said we had a few more stops and six hours before we would reach our new home. My children wanted to stretch their legs, and it was time for my injection; so they stood outside the bus, and my daughter administered the medicine in my forearm.

When everyone returned to their seats on the bus, I noticed the bus had inmates of different cultures. There were Laotians, Guatemalans, Kenyans, Japanese, and Mexicans—apparently poverty was not discriminative. My twins in my lap with my older children in the seats behind us, I pressed my head onto the glass of the barred window listening to the engine of the bus until my consciousness returned to the trial.

Supercilious was confident that she could prove and win her case, so she offered me a list of pleas that could make my life sentence manageable to deal with before my guilty verdict was rendered. Disgusted by Supercilious's arrogance, Grace assured me, " You have time to find employment, remain hopeful everything is going to work out," he said with unfeigned certainty.

Yet year after year, I never gained employment; every employer closed their door of opportunity to me because I was either overqualified or my credit score failed to reach their ideal altitude. Finally, I arrived home with hurt feet and no pride from all the rejections of the day. Walking into the door, I saw my lottery number televised with an announcement that my family was to report immediately to No Where. Grace must have seen that my number was up because he called my home leaving a fountain of encouraging words that flowed from his tongue, flooding my answering machine. He said, "I am still in this fight with you." What fight? I thought. The battle was lost.

Two days later, I received a letter in the mail that stated, in eight months my family and I would be bused to a prison located between Maryland and Virginia, 1,200 miles away from Kansas City, Kansas.

After hours of riding on the bus, I woke up with cramps in my legs and a nauseated feeling like we were on a rollercoaster as the tires of our rusted white school bus went up and down every pothole on the street. Looking into the red haze of my children's eyes, I could see the fear in their hearts. I observed that the bus was overcrowded with more inmates since our last stop in Hardin, all sharing one commonality, one fear—prison.

Entering Freedom City, there were two stone buildings that stood like guards on the outskirts of the city with blinking blue and green fluorescent-lit signs that read FOODY and LIFE OR DEATH EMERGENCY HOSPITAL. The driver drove for miles from the two buildings passing tall houses, small shacks, huge dumpsters, and gas stations before I saw a courtyard that enclosed a huge house with chest-high bushes as its border. Written on the house were the words OLD LIBRARY, and then the driver turned left onto Division Street.

Hard breathing, whispering in many languages, and children crying became the melody of terror from the inmates as we neared our destination. Division Street had a forest of trees on the left side and creepy shadows of unidentifiable objects stationed near the biggest trees. I presumed we would know what the objects were in the morning light. The driver interrupted my thought of creepy shadows with a screeching sound of what rubber remained of the tires, concluding our rollercoaster ride with an abrupt stop. Outside the window was a graveyard of cells in rows that resembled a tomb plot arrangement. We arrived at the prison in the middle of the night, exhausted from the ride and disappointment about my verdict. I breathed in and out the air that used to be free, and now it's the air of captivity. All the inmates peeked through the windows at seasoned inmates wearing white jumpers walking around the entrance of the prison, chatting and gawking at our bus. The bus stopped at the bottom of what looked like a hill of cells linked together by a fence and barbwire for decor. The endless rows of cells were on both sides of a street named Valley. Many guards came running to greet us separated by their uniform colors of yellow, gray, and white, led by one woman.

"Good Evening, good evening, good evening, I am your appointed keeper, you will call me Lady Lost," shouted the short lady. "My job is to make sure everyone becomes cold and stiff around here, and I haven't had one complaint from the government nor the inmates," she said sternly with a smile. "Please pay attention to me when I am speaking because I detest repetition. Before you exit the buses, you will gather your kids and your belongings from the rear. I expect all of you to align yourselves adjacent to the bus you arrived on, maintaining order as there are two busloads of inmates delivered here tonight."

"Cold and stiff, does that mean there is no way out of here?" one of the inmates openly asked other inmates inside the bus, but no one responded.

My children proceeded to follow Lady Lost's instructions without uttering a questioning word to me. Content, my eldest daughter, placed a huge box of injections in my hand before grabbing a bag and exiting the bus. Content makes certain that I inject my medicine timely. She is my most responsible child.

"As you may have noticed, there is a cell of five homes in one row," Lady Lost continued. "This first cell, I call Registration, it has one way to enter and one way to exit. Now, you will enter on the South end of Registration, there you will receive your jumpers, food allowance for the month, and identity papers. Please do not lose your identity papers because they are irreplaceable since you've been exiled from America."

As Lady Lost continued to yell instructions her short stature bounced with each bellow of her voice. "You will exit from the North end of Registration, which leads to the street. There you will be greeted with a team of officers that match your jumper. Each group of officers will be referenced by their team names. Officers dressed in yellow will be referred to as Officer Future, officers dressed in gray will be referred to as Officer Present, and the officers dressed in white are referred to as, you may already have guessed, Officer Past. None of the officers will conduct themselves informally with you, so there is no need to know their identity," Lady Lost proceeded to howl as she stepped onto two large rocks in an effort to make herself visible to the inmates standing in the back, closest to the bus.

While Lady Lost recited her soliloquy of prison rules, an old woman with short black hair wearing a white jumper peeked around the corner of Registration studying the new inmates like a rat studies humans before sneaking to steal our leftover crumbs. This woman pressed her wide shaped body on the side of Registration where only her head could be seen by the officers. She apparently did not want her survey of the new inmates to be detected by Lady Lost. My assessment of her wrinkled face and green eyes didn't last long because she realized her presence was not covert and hobbled quickly out of my sight.

"You will be called by your name because it sounds better than inmate letters written on your jumper," continued Lady Lost. "Your cells are bilevel townhomes like this first one, except there are inner walls that separate each townhome for the family's minimal privacy. I know Americans refer to this place as a prison, cells, or jail, but I like to think of them as townhomes. This is my big town composed of many homes, again, it just sounds better to the ears. Now, let's get you, new residents, registered, so you can get acquainted with your new homes," Lady Lost said with no enthusiasm.

"This will never be your home, it is a prison, a prison of cells," I muttered to my five children standing in line around me.

Receiving some assistance to descend from the rocks, Lady Lost took her place at the door presenting identity papers to the new inmates while the working residents inside presented assigned jumpers and food allowance. Lady Lost asked every inmate their first and last name as she shuffled through her folder in search of their identity papers. A woman and three children were ahead of us as the inmates hesitantly stepped forward in the line.

"What is your name?" Lady Lost asked the woman.

"My name is Ms. Deceitful Ways, and these are my children, Jealousy, Lethargic, and Fear," the woman answered. Deceitful stood in line with perfect posture as if she was preparing to model on a runway. Her kids' demeanor was that of children's entitlement to their mother's throne of adoration. She had long hair that moved with each step she took and a smile that bewitched men and was the envy of women. Ms. Deceitful Ways knew she was beautiful, and she knew how to use her beauty.

This beautiful woman in front of us made me wonder why she was in prison with us and not in America. I guess poverty has no respect for the vanities in a person or higher education, I thought.

"Only answer what I ask, your papers will reveal the rest, and your rehearsed smile will get you nothing here," said Lady Lost.

Speaking to the residents inside, Lady Lost assigned Ms. Deceitful Ways and her children gray jumpers before she told them to wait outside. "Next!" she yelled. "What's your name?" Lady Lost asked looking at me with squinted eyes as if I violated one of her rules.

"Positively Chose, but I prefer Positive," I replied.

Laughing, she turned to speak with officers Past, "This girl thinks I care what she prefers. My only care is money and each dollar I make on the cold and stiff. She doesn't know that here, but she will. No one cares or at least they shouldn't about what anyone prefers in prison. Does she know where she is?" Lady Lost questioned the silent officers Past as if I was one of her dreadful portraits mounted on the wall behind her, unable to hear her conversation.

Returning her attention to me, Lady Lost began yelling again, "I'm going to say this one last time so everyone had better hear me, or pass my words to those who can't. When you talk to me, you will answer only what I ask you and nothing more. If you decide to give me more information than what is requested of you, I will reduce your food allowance for the month." Then squinting at me, she reported, "It reads here on your papers that you're sentenced to life in No Where, and you didn't accept a plea from one of my favorite prosecutors, Ms. Supercilious. Why didn't you take a plea?" she inquired.

"I am not a criminal," I replied.

"Hum," Lady Lost groaned. "It also reads that you have five children. Do you have all five of your children here, no one got left behind, correct?" questioned Lady Lost.

"No one was left behind, they're all here," I answered. Content, Strength, Peace, Truth, and Reason were standing in birth order directly behind me with Truth and Reason peering around Peace to get a closer look at Lady Lost.

"Good, good, big families are highly profitable when they're cold and stiff. What is that box you're holding?" asked Lady Lost.

"It is a box of injections for my illness," I responded.

"Well, those will remain here in the refrigerator. You may get them as you need them," she said before she began to holler again. "If there are any other inmates who need refrigeration for their medication, you will surrender the medicine here. Only the Valley residents are permitted to use drugs unsupervised." Then she confiscated my box of medication and assigned us yellow jumpers and gave me a $200 food voucher. We exited Registration onto Valley Street as official residents of the prison.

2

There were a lot of officers. Most of them were tall, some had short hair, a few had long hair, and the rest were bald. Lady lost must not like women too much, I thought, because all of the officers were male. Lining up behind officers Future, we stood there in silence holding our garbage bags while we waited on the rest of the inmates to complete registration. We could see white jumpers walking everywhere as the night air became cooler with each hour. The residents wearing the white jumpers appeared to have something wrong with their minds. Some would approach the lines closely then run away laughing, some jumped rope with the pavement as they leaped from the sidewalk to the street and back again, while others allowed the darkness to profile their jumpers as they stared at us mumbling to each other.

"Momma, we don't have to live next to them do we?" asked Peace. Peace is my ten-year-old son who asks rhetorical questions that are often on the minds of everyone.

"No, smarter than me, we have to wear the yellow jumpers," whispered Strength. Strength is my twelve-year-old daughter who sarcastically speaks the truth to anyone, adult or child, without dismay even if no one was talking to her.

"What time is it, Momma? You know you have to take your medicine," nagged Content.

"Be quiet, just be quiet all of you, everything in time" I whispered.

Finally, Lady Lost exited Registration, with quick small strides in a rush to lead her officers and new residents on a tour through No Where. She intended to rid herself of the new inmates for the night.

"You will find a letter at the head of your identity papers, this letter is your assigned townhome," she informed. "All of the residents with white jumpers will remain here in the Valley. Officers Past will be monitoring your area all day and night, especially at night. There is no one to call for help, so don't run to officers Past with your problems. They are only here to make sure all residents are accounted for," Lady Lost said with annoyance as if many inmates ask for help from officers Past in spite of her rule.

"Momma, the lady said there is no help here. What are we going to do if we need help?" asked Peace.

Before I could open my mouth, Lady Lost answered Peace's question, "There is no help, just a phone in Registration that we use to receive calls. I make the only outgoing calls from my office to the hospital on behalf of my residents. We have one hospital that you saw on your way into Freedom City, it read Life or Death Emergency Room, and it's used only if there is a chance you will become cold and stiff prematurely." Lady Lost giggled. "There is no help little boy, absolutely no help" she yelled before returning to her rehearsed tour. "There is no night curfew in the Valley, only wakeup announcements by officers Past at 4 a.m. and outside call at 6 a.m.

We kept walking up the hill as inmates began withdrawing themselves from our group to deposit their children and their belongings into their respective townhomes. After a mile of walking we arrived to the section of townhomes that claimed the gray jumper inmates. There were no inmates outside, but there were inmates peeking out of their windows at us. It was so silent that it reminded me of the solitude I found on my mother's wide concrete porch under the full moon's ray. Already I loathed being in Freedom and wanted desperately to return to America.

"These townhomes are supervised by officers Present. The street name has changed from Valley to Effort Street midway between all of the townhomes," Lady Lost pointed out. "The mailbox is underneath this one streetlight with the intercom that looks alone in the darkness. The gray jumper residents including the yellow jumper residents have a curfew at 6 p.m., with a wakeup time of 4 a.m., and outside call at 6am. Often times you will see the gray jumpers either relocate to the Valley or Effort Street while you live here, that is their decision alone to make or not, some choose to remain in the gray jumpers for life."

The group dwindled to three families as we walked further up Effort Street behind Lady Lost and her officers Future. "Here is your new home for the rest of you residents. If you look down past the Present townhomes, you can see way down into the darkness of the Past townhomes where you arrived. It's not the best view, but it's a view," said Lady Lost.

"Momma, we live on top of a hill like a castle," whispered Strength.

"We don't live here, we're just visiting the castle," I said lowly. My children fascinate me because they are filled with the wonder of their imaginations and the despair of my disappointment, yet they share my disappointment for less than a second before they return to the exciting adventure in their imaginations of no care and no worries for the future because the future doesn't exist to their present freedom of childhood play.

Disgusted by the illusion of this place ever being a castle, Lady Lost continued, "Effort Street has an exit from No Where into Freedom City. If you recall, there were two signs that read, "FOODY" and "Life or Death Hospital". FOODY supplies the prison with your meals needed for the week every Friday. While, the Life or Death Hospital is used for the cold and stiff only. I'm sure you noticed that there are homes, gas stations, and dumpsters that surround us, making up our precious Freedom City, when you entered Freedom State on the bus," mentioned Lady Lost. "Don't worry yourselves with trying to run away because the people of Freedom City don't take kindly to outsiders, and your jumpers will identify where you belong," she added. "You all are dismissed from my sight for a couple of hours, but be listening to that intercom you saw midway through here as I will make further announcements soon," she yelled as she walked away, and her height became even smaller as she descended Effort Street.

The officers Future were in a strict formation as they waited in the street for us to find our assigned townhome. "Momma, your paper work read 'townhome C,' right?" asked Content with a puzzled look on her face as she glanced over the letters on the cells.

"Yes, we are assigned to cell C," I answered.

Truth and Reason ran down the rows of townhomes looking for C. "We found it, it's over here, Momma!" they yelled in unison. Truth and Reason are my fraternal twin boys who seemed to be excited and happy all the time even when our conditions were in no state of happiness. I think when a child is barely over the age of five, they exist in their boundless dreams of divine happiness before they're awaken by the realities of poverty.

All five of them piled into the cell behind me with our garbage bags as Peace closed the door. Standing there in awe, we saw the door automatically seal the bolt lock into place with a loud noise. "Momma, did you see that?" asked Peace with anxiety in his voice.

"Of course, we all saw that," replied Strength as she comforted the twins by distracting them with toys from their garbage bags. My children stood in silence on the moonlit moving checkerboard floor of tile, waiting for me to speak, but I was too tired to say anything uplifting. Silently walking to the left of the room with my children on my heels, I found a light against the wall; and after our eyes adjusted to the illumination, I saw a staircase straight ahead, when my children began to dance in one place, stomping bugs to death on the floor, filling the cell with screams of horror.

"Bugs," Truth and Reason pointed to the floor.

"Roa-ches, ma-ny roaches!" stuttered Peace in so much fear that he wanted to run to me, forgetting he was standing next to me causing himself to fall on the moving floor, terror in his eyes.

"Bunch of babies," exclaimed Strength as she stomped roaches to death with her left and right foot, the rhythm pounding the floor. The faster the bugs moved, the more she stomped.

"That explains why the floor moved," I said, walking through the entrance of the next room looking for a light with more caution than I did the first time. The next room had a stove underneath the light switch I turned on, with a connected counter and silver sink made of discolored aluminum and tin. Across from the section of clean dishes was a small refrigerator that was barely cold inside with enough space to hold two dinner plates, a gallon of milk, and three bottles of water.

"This is the kitchen? How are we going to refrigerate food when your medicine will take up most of the space?" asked Content.

"Remember, Lady Lost took Momma's injections and stored them in Registration," Strength answered proudly, "so we should have plenty of room for food in the refrigerator."

"Forget the food. Do you see all these bugs? These bugs are going to eat our food when we sleep. Look, they are crawling on the countertops and walls like we're the unwelcomed pests in the kitchen. Momma, where are we supposed to sleep or eat in this place?" groaned Peace, shaking the roaches off his clothes. With no answer for the questions my older children were asking, I followed the twins upstairs. Finding another light switch on the wall near the bathroom, I saw moving walls inside two rooms parallel to the bathroom. The twins walked slowly into one of the two rooms wanting to compete for locating a light switch before me, instantly remembering how terrified of bugs they are, they decided to wait for me to find the light. In each room there were so many roaches scrambling frantically to hide from the light that I felt nauseated watching them crawl over each other. There were two cots with old mattresses on top of them that held a stack of blankets, sheets, and towels neatly folded and placed on the corner of each mattress resembling two islands in the midst of an ocean of roaches.

"Mommy," called the twins.

"Yes," I answered.

"Can we sleep standing?"

"No, you cannot sleep standing. It is better to lay on the springs of these mattresses with a few roaches then lose your balance in a dream and fall into most of the roaches on the floor," I assured them of my reasoning for my answer as I heard my older children's footsteps on the stairs.

"Strength, Peace, don't look in there," warned Truth greeting them at the top of the stairs.

"That's where momma says we have to sleep with the creepy roaches on the bed because it's better than falling on the crawly roaches on the floor," Reason added with confidence that he understood what I explained.

My older children were speechless at the presentation of their sleeping quarters. "We have to sleep in here? There are only four cots, where you sleeping, Momma?" asked Peace.

"With us, with us, Mommy is sleeping with us," cheered Truth and Reason.

"They're excited about sleeping here?" mumbled Strength to Content.

"No, the twins are excited about Momma sleeping with them," answered Content rolling her eyes disapprovingly to Strength's question before she headed downstairs to retrieve the rest of our bags.

My children continued to talk to me and ask me endless questions about our problems for which I had no answer. I stared at the raggedy condition of the cell in disgust and thought this is not home, this is not home, repeating the words while ignoring their little voices of our shared complaints. Then a loud sound of pounding on the door startled me, intruding on my thoughts of the filth and unlivable conditions of this cell. Officers Future announced, "4 a.m. wakeup call."

"Already, it's wakeup call? I haven't had a bath, and we haven't put away anything yet," complained Content searching through her bag of toiletries.

"Where is my toothbrush?" asked Peace.

"Everything we have is in the garbage bags, Peace. Strength, clean the twins and get them dressed in the jumpers, please," I instructed.

"What are we going to eat?" announced Truth like he spoke through a bull horn.

"I'm hungry," agreed Reason to Truth's question.

"Have patience, everyone, please. You have spent the past thirty minutes talking, and no one is moving in the direction of being prepared to leave the cell for the day. I can't deal with all of this right now. Your complaining is doing nothing for my sanity. You see where we're at, and you are bothering me with what you know, you all know good hygiene is a must. Look, if you need to be clean before leaving, then do so, bathe, brush your teeth, comb your hair, get dressed into the jumpers, whatever, but stop talking, please, stop talking," I begged. Lady Lost will do enough talking for all of us when she gives her announcements, My children were stunned at my tone and began moving quickly to prepare themselves to see the cells in the daylight.

At five minutes before 6 a.m., the bolts released and officers Future were yelling, "Outside call, outside call," from Effort Street. Peace opened the door to the blinding sun light and stepped outside. Each child followed Peace into the morning sky, and I was the last to exit closing the door. *Boom, clank, clink*, the bolted lock sealed again as we stepped down off the doorstep and lined up on the three-block sidewalk from the doorstep. With better light I could see these town-homes were made from leftover building materials that were presumably used to build the better homes outside the prison.

"Good morning, morning, morning, said a familiar voice from the intercom on the streetlight pole. This is the morning announcement, so listen up. We have several families that have joined us here in No Where last night, and they are not familiar with all the rules. So listen up as I detest the waist of energy used to repeat myself," said the voice of Lady Lost.

"Isn't that the second time she's used the world 'detest'? asked Peace to Content. "I thought she didn't like to repeat herself."

Content refused to play the game of answering Peace's questions he knows the answers to, so she astutely listened to the intercom for any new rules. Lady Lost continued, "The new residents have just experienced the first rule: timeliness. I told them the schedule of No Where a few hours ago. Now, that you've noticed the doors automatically lock, if you are not in or out of your townhome on time, the officers will manually unlock the door and bring you to me. Keep this in the front of your mind at all times, I don't like unexpected visits from residents.

"Next rule, you will remain outside of your townhome for twelve hours. I don't care what you do or where you go, but you're not entering the townhome before the twelve hours have expired or sundown. Since you were too lazy to be profitable citizens in America daily, you will be outside the townhome daily as I detest laziness.

"There she goes again, Momma, did you hear that? She said 'detest' again," Peace pointed out to his amusement.

"The Foody Truck will be here today. It arrives here every Friday of every week with your groceries. Use your vouchers and purchase what you can afford." Then the intercom went silent. I guess Lady Lost isn't big on salutations, just repeating herself.

Sitting down on the step with my back resting against the door of the cell, I watched the twins practice their letter recognition and phonics. "NW-EH-P" pointed out Reason on Truth's jumper. Then, Reason turned his back to Truth, and read "NW-EHP", laughing together in confidence of knowing their alphabets.

"What do the letters stand for?" asked Content.

"They are some sort of an acronym for this place," I answered.

My children stood around looking at other families with yellow jumpers while waiting on me to give them instructions. Honestly, I had no instructions to give, no plan, but to sit and observe nature for twelve hours. These birds in front of me who were standing at earth's table having breakfast until they flew into the trees.

"Momma, what we supposed to do all day?" Strength asked while watching other kids being sociable with each other.

"You're not supposed to ask Momma any more questions," replied Content as she watched me sit with my back against the door under the sun, tapping the heel of my shoe on the pavement. The sun grew brighter with each minute of the morning, casting my shadow slowly over the townhomes across from us. The prison children grew restless and bored with racing each other, and pulling up what was left of the grass patch in front of their cells. Strength and Content whispered about the different cultures of people they saw who didn't speak English. Peace observed how the men walked mimicking what he saw. He curled his arms in the form of the letter C as if his arms were muscular walking a few steps forward in the grass patch. Then, he turned to walk toward me poking his belly out, trying to shape it into a ball that he perceived another man was carrying in his stomach.

With my eyes closed, listening to Truth and Reason laugh about getting dirty from digging a hole in the ground with sticks; I pretended we could live in the dark space I saw under my eyelids where poverty and prison couldn't find us, until I heard that dreadful voice announcing my name over the intercom.

3

"Positive, I repeat, Positive, please report to Registration, you have a phone call," broadcasted Lady Lost through the intercom. Disturbed from my hideout meditation underneath my eyelids, I rose up, dusted my jumper off, and proceeded to walk toward Registration for the phone. The gray jumper residents whispered my name and pointed at my children who walked so close to me that I dare not attempt any direction but forward if I didn't want a domino fall of kids. As we approached Registration, each step grew louder. Men where banging on the doors of their townhomes demanding entrance. Women were vomiting outside their townhomes from some kind of poison the night before. Paper, empty bottles, needles, mail, and broken glass were scattered down the sidewalks and the street. Trash, lots of trash, I saw trash everywhere that the night sky did not take a snapshot of when we stepped down from the bus last night.

There were more children in the Valley near Registration than on Effort Street. These children were playing in unclean white jumpers without a care in the world, and my twins tugged so hard on my jumper wanting to join them in the fun.

Before I entered Registration I spoke with my kids, "Everyone stand in the grass away from the sidewalk so the traffic of other residents can flow in and out of Registration with ease." Leaving my nervous children outside, I opened the door, a male resident ushered me to the phone whispering, "Use it quickly." When I touched the handle of the phone, Lady Lost came from behind me, placing her hand firmly on top of mine. "All calls are recorded," she said looking sternly into my eyes before entering into her office directly across from the mounted phone on the wall.

"Hello."

"Hello, Positive?" the male voice asked.

"Speaking," I responded.

"This is Grace, your attorney. Are you and the kids okay?"

"Are you serious? Did you just ask me if we were okay?" I asked rhetorically. "I did everything you told me to do, you never heard any murmuring from me for years during my trial. I followed your advice, my attorney's advice all the way to a family life sentence in prison, and you're asking me if we're okay!" I yelled through the phone.

"I understand you're upset, maybe even distraught by the verdict, but I haven't left your side in this, I've always been here with you every step of the way," said Grace redundantly.

"What side? There is no side, in case you weren't paying attention when the jury rendered their decision, allow me to refresh your memory of their verdict: guilty. They said I am guilty, guilty, and guilty after the courts made me relive my embarrassing mistakes that I made in my personal life, humiliating me on the witness stand, never questioning me about my family and peers and the endless testimonials of my character and academic accomplishments, and they still rendered a guilty verdict. There are no more sides Grace, it's over. We've been banished to No Where for life!" I yelled into a screamed high pitch on the phone.

"Positive, please try to calm down. Breathe, focus on inhaling slowly for ten seconds, then exhale for ten seconds, that should give me enough time to speak uninterrupted," suggested Grace. I looked up at the dirty ceiling and began breathing while he spoke. "I know that being incarcerated with your family is unbearable for you. I know that you worked hard and followed all of my instructions during these past five years to demonstrate your productiveness as an American citizen, and the jury found you guilty anyway. With all that we both know happened, I'm asking you to allow me more time with your case. Will you continue to allow me to guide you through your unfortunate circumstance? I just need more time, and I need you to wait on me while I help you. I will help you, Positive."

"You guided us to prison, now you want the privilege of guiding us straight to hell, is that it?" I asked pretentiously. "Now you say you need more time, you have wasted enough of my time and my children's time every step of the way, of every year for the past five years," I said gritting my teeth. I noticed that the male resident was making some sort of motion to me, pointing at his wrist.

"I'm sorry Grace, where are my manners, my mother raised me better than this, thank you for being beside me doing nothing but advising me to become an educated prisoner. Is there anything else you wanted? Why did you call me, Grace?" I demanded.

"I called because I want you to wait for me to handle this in your life and the lives of your children. I'm not done yet Positive. I need you to trust me. I know you were found guilty and it's devastating. I know you are angry at me, but I just ask that you do this last thing and wait with a bit more patience, please," he asked sounding so sure of himself, like he did in court.

"I'm out of time on the phone, and I'm all out of patience. Tell you what, you wait, you watch and wait for me to deteriorate in this place because that's all I'm in the mood to do right now," I said. Lady Lost ended her eavesdropping at the same time I decided there was nothing left to say and we hung up the receivers together.

The male resident whispered, "She was eavesdropping on your call, next time keep it short and sweet."

"I don't care, I don't care anymore about anything," I said to him as I felt my words tattooing themselves on my heart. Exiting Registration and picking up my twins, I began my march up to Effort Street.

We had passed two rows of cells before my kids saw the hobbling woman holding a bag approaching us. The twins wiggled down out of my arms and ran to receive the bag.

"Was that lady talking to herself before she saw us?" asked Peace.

"Maybe she was organizing her thoughts for what she wanted to say when she saw us," replied Content, "keep your voice down with your questions, you heard Momma screaming, and it's not good for her health," she reminded Peace.

"No, that lady was talking to herself, she answered somebody named Love," insisted Peace watching the twins greet the lady and receive the bags. The woman did not receive the smiles from the twins. Instead of speaking to them, she threw them the bag quickly and hobbled away mumbling something.

"Maybe she had to go to the bathroom and couldn't hold it long enough to say hi," Strength chimed in on the conversation. "What's in the bag?" Strength inquired of the twins.

"It's our bag, it's our bag, it's our bag," sang the twins keeping the items hidden from Strength as they ran to climb into my arms. Marching halfway up the hill, I held the twins and their bag while my older children debated about whether or not the hobbling white jumper was a crazy woman or not.

Almost dropping the twins and the bag, we collided with another family dressed in gray jumpers. "Excuse us, my two kids love to play everywhere we go. We didn't mean to almost knock you down," pardoned the woman. My name is Escape, and those were my two children running down the hill: my son, Praise, and my daughter, Harmony."

Escape is the same height as me with brown dusty hair that reached her ear in length. She has a scar on her face that resembled a crescent moon. Escape smiled with every word she spoke even if I didn't understand it for the weak foreign accent that appeared in her speech.

Dismissing Escape's cheerful greeting, I caught my balance just before I fell on top of my twins and proceeded to march up the hill like this woman didn't say a word to me. "Nice to meet you," Peace acknowledged the woman.

"Momma, why didn't you speak to that nice lady back there?" asked Strength.

"Because I don't have to speak to her or anyone else here, I don't owe anyone anything, not even acknowledgement that they exist," breathlessly the words seeped out while my body's energy burned in my legs and arms from carrying my twin's dead weight. "You don't know that woman, so how do you know she is nice?" I asked Strength.

"She is the only one who has greeted us since we moved here," reasoned Strength.

"Can't you recognize when Momma is asking a rhetorical question, she did not want an answer to her question," stated Peace to Strength. Finally we arrived at cell C, utterly exhausted. I sat down wishing the weather was colder. It really wasn't as cold as it should have been for November weather, and the sky didn't appear to be cloudy either. The day was oddly sunny for a state centered between Virginia and Maryland. Other residents were enjoying the day without us. They were playing music from their portable radios, kids were chasing each other, and every couple of hours we would see a different car drive through No Where from the Valley and exit out here on Effort Street heading North. No cars were ever seen going south.

"Truth and Reason, tell Mommy what you have in your bag?" I asked.

"We don't know," the twins answered while taking items out of the bag.

Confiscating the bag from the twins, Strength found eight insect and rodent plug-ins, Pine-Sol, bleach, dishwashing soap, and a lighter. "Why did the strange lady give us these items?" Strength asked.

Not answering her questions, I sat in silence not wanting to think anymore. I appreciate what the stranger gave us, but that's as far as I wanted to think about it. Staring into space straight ahead, glancing at the leaves that remain on the trees, I just wanted to be left alone, alone to be nonexistent to my children, to No Where, to myself, for five minutes.

"I'm hungry," protested Strength. "Momma, what are we going to eat?"

"They gave us food vouchers, so we should be getting food eventually, it is Friday," Content responded.

"Everyone else is eating around us. Look over there, that man and his family are eating peanut butter and jelly sandwiches, and that lady is snacking on fruit with her kids, and no one is waiting to spend no stupid vouchers," argued Strength. In the middle of her statement, I heard a tire crush a piece of glass in the street. I heard awful music playing on a loud speaker from a vehicle that reminds of an ice-cream delivery truck. It was a rusty truck, with dents and groves that bordered the name FOODY. It sounded like a military tank traveling up Effort Street.

"Momma, I'll go with Content and pick out the food," offered Peace.

"You keep track of the twins," Content instructed Strength.

Twenty minutes had passed since Content and Peace left to cash in the food vouchers. We sat outside the cell with our stomachs doing the talking as we waited for them to return. The sun remained on the west side of the cells playing peekaboo behind each set of clouds that passed. It was almost Lady Lost's cell time call when Content and Peace returned to us with bags of food smiling. "Momma, we bought fruit, bread, noodles, water, and a gallon of milk," Peace reported.

"Why didn't you buy some meat?" asked Strength.

"The delivery guy said meat was too expensive for our vouchers at the end of the month. He said we have to buy meat at the beginning of the month when our vouchers are worth more," explained Content looking at the twins bouncing up and down.

"Mommy, I have to go to the bathroom," said Reason.

"Me too," added Truth.

"Don't worry, Momma, I'll take them to that outhouse I saw on our way up from Registration," said Content.

"No you won't, Momma said we can't use public toilets," protested Peace.

"Then why don't you let them pee on Peace's feet, and he can hold it for them until we go inside," smirked Strength.

"Would ya'll shut up, can't you see Momma isn't well, just shut up," pleaded Content. "I will take them over to the bushes, they're boys. They can stand and let it out. Momma, did you get your shot from Registration today?"

"No, I forgot. Peace, run with me down the hill so I can get my medicine. Strength and Content stay here, don't leave this cell, and don't speak to anyone." Peace and I jogged toward Registration passing by the residential onlookers staring at us like they were watching a marathon. Peace waited outside Registration, and I went after my medication.

"You know Registration is about to close, and Lady Lost is preparing to announce Inside call soon," said the male resident I saw earlier when I had a phone call.

"I'm here for my injection."

"It's right here on the desk. I read the box and placed it here for you. You know you're late at remembering your medicine for someone who has such a serious illness," he said like we were family and he had permission to chastise me.

"My name is Deliverance. Don't worry about introducing yourself. I remember you and your children from last night. Listen, none of these residents put your family in No Where, so stop acting like you're upset with us. In this place you're going to need a friend," he warned.

"Deliverance, is it? Thanks for having my injection ready when I came in. I'm not here to be anyone's friend, so I could care less about your perception of me. Take care of yours, and I will take care of mine." Grabbing my injection and exiting Registration from a nosey man, my son and I ran up the hill. As we were running, we heard an ear-disturbing loud sound from the intercom, and I heard officers jogging in formation behind us. Then Lady Lost's voice began to compete with the noisy intercom as she gave instructions of which I could not hear clearly over my drumming heart rate beating in our hurry to return to #C.

"Valley residents, these instructions are not for you. Effort Street residents, pay attention," ordered Lady Lost. My officers are nearing your townhomes to relieve the current Officers from their post until tomorrow. All of the residents must return to their townhomes while these Officer exchanges occur. To the new residents, if you should hear screams in the night or see shattered glass on the ground in the morning, do not be alarmed, this is the norm around here. The Valley residents are known to be destructive at night. Also, you should hear these sounds in the distance of your townhomes, but in case you hear it closer, then it means my officers had to intervene, so you should stand away from the windows of your homes. Last, but not least, inside call," Lady Lost stopped her announcements abruptly.

Peace and I could see my children entering in the townhome as we neared the door. Sweating and profusely tired, Peace grabbed my hand for the last steps and we slid into the door. Strength slammed it shut and it sealed for the night.

My children were all accounted for while Peace and I stood with our hands above our heads inhaling as much air as the cell had to offer. At the age of thirty-two, I couldn't believe how exhausted I was from a simple one mile jog. I was worn out. With Truth and Reason resting their heads on my legs, they felt like dumbbells making my legs burn more. I wanted them to get off of me, but they remembered all the bugs that surrounded them and tried to leap into my arms insisting on being lifted from the floor immediately.

"Uggh, I hate coming in here," Peace groaned.

"We have some plugins now, and they cause the bugs to go into the ground through some sound it makes in the wall," Content described as she read the label.

"Uh, I'm going to be sick," Strength moaned just before she vomited on the moving floor.

"That's nasty," the twins said as they examined Strength's vomit from the view of my arms.

"Listen to me," I said firmly, "I don't want any complaining tonight. I don't want to hear another word from any of you. If there is the slightest inference of a complaint coming from your thought, leave it in your mind. Peace, get some towels from the beds upstairs and help Strength clean up her mess. Truth and Reason, follow Peace upstairs and sit on the beds until the food is ready. Content, put the plugins in any wall sockets you find in this place, one in every room preferably," I instructed.

My feet were headed into the kitchen when all of the bugs began scattering and running over each other in a hurry to leave the cell in any direction they could after Content inserted one plugin. Wanting to scream at the top of her lungs, Content made every effort to complete her assignment in silence as she distorted her facial expression to resemble the horror she felt as she stepped on bugs toward the next outlet. Ordinarily I would have been grossed out, but being disgusted by bugs takes energy that I don't have since running in the Olympics five minutes ago.

We spent several hours cleaning the cell, creating a meal, and bathing before my children were finally in the bed, leaving me to the silence I desired. Lying on the cold tile floor with no blankets and the last of the roaches that couldn't find the ground exit to this place, I stared at the ceiling. In that moment, my lips started moving, and my voice surfaced from my soul as it began to moan into a conversation of honesty with space and time because I couldn't be speaking to God.

God has closed his ears to the soundwaves of my voice that used to pierce the floors of heaven before we were sentenced to this place. "Why me?" I asked whispering, holding my poverty papers in my hands. Pondering on what could have gone wrong in the case. Was it Grace's fault, was he a lawyer who made Cs in law school? Did he know all along, that I would end up in No Where no matter what I did? Why is he trying to build my hope again, when hope has deserted me? Better yet, was there anything that I could have done alone, without Grace, or differently that would have persuaded the jury that I belonged in America? I'm a rehabilitated American citizen from having a high school diploma to acquiring a bachelor's degree, I'm one of them now, I am an educated American.

I sat in silence waiting on an answer to my questions from space and time, the roaches, from somewhere, anywhere, knowing my answers would never come. My mind emptied itself of any leftover hope, drained from useless motivation to prevent the inevitable prison and raising my children here. Neglected by space and time, I stared at the wall until the hue of the room changed from black, to gray, to blue. It's about 4 o'clock in the morning, and I hear the security guards waking up the residents like an alarm that never breaks. No one has to wake me up because I can't sleep in this place.

4

"Momma, why do they have to yell wake up, why can't they knock on the doors like normal people?" Strength asked. "We hear their loud opinions of us every morning and night as they stand like statutes keeping a watch on everybody's house every day. They could knock. We're not strangers to each other anymore!" yelled Strength from the top of the stairs.

"Don't ever call this place our house, this is prison, and a jail is never home" I lectured in response to Strength while making them some sandwiches for lunch. All my children ran around in preparation to leave the cell. The twins waited to be dressed. Peace and Strength argued over the bathroom time, and Content cleaned their rooms to keep the bugs from revisiting. I managed to take a shower with the twins playing in my sprinkles as the water bounced off of me hitting their little hands at the bottom of the tub. Then Content chased them out of the bathroom to give me some privacy. Strength ironed her jumper as she is gravely annoyed by wrinkles in clothing, and Peace gathered the lunch bags from the kitchen counter. They were ready and excited for the 6 a.m. outside call, ready to do nothing and be nothing in No Where.

I opened the door to the brightest light of the morning. What was the sun doing out in November? Is it going to be this bright every day, shinning on our despair? I wondered. I would prefer that misty fog revisit the air. Stiff, wet branches and heavy gray with a bit of white in the heavens, a type of weather that shares my thoughts of no clarity about what storm is to approach in the later days of this weekend. Annoyed with the weather's happiness, I took my seat in front of my cell and watched my children anticipate other children to exiting their cells.

"It seems like the sun adores No Where this year," a distant voice said. Lifting my head slightly gazing between my children's shoes, I saw the same woman who almost knocked me down two days ago quickly approaching us with her two children. I am not looking to make friends in this place, I don't want to exist, nor do anything in this place, so she'll have to find someone else to bother because I'm not in the mood were my thoughts.

"The sun is so happy today, matter of fact, it's been so happy every day this winter. Has it forgotten what season it is?" She asked looking at my kids before searching for my face behind my children's soldier-like stance. "Good morning, my name is Escape, in case you've forgotten from the other day."

"That is not what you said as though you are repeating yourself to a deaf person. You said, 'It seems like the Sun adores No Where this year,'" I corrected her. "Yes, I know your name is Escape and your children's names are Praise and Harmony. You can stop right there, that's close enough," I instructed, preventing Escape from seeing me as I leaned my head back on the cell, remaining hidden behind my children. "What do you want?" I asked as a voice projecting from the ground, peeking through the legs of my children.

"Wow, I never met a friend like you who doesn't speak to strangers face to face, huh?" Escape asked rhetorically. "I know this is your first time being in No Where, and I'm certain it's your first time being in Freedom City since I saw your arrival here from the bus the other night, so I'm here to be friendly and neighborly by taking you and your children on a walk with us through Freedom City today," replied Escape.

"We're not friends, and I'm not interested in seeing your Freedom City. We are not the only people who arrived here the other night, go show your hospitality to someone else," I insisted from behind my children who were still silently standing like soldiers prepared for war in case Escape should prove to be bothersome to me.

"If you insist that we leave you alone, no problem, but before I do, you should consider this: you are in a strange place, and you don't know anyone or where to go around here when you finally get out of your mind of depression. I'm offering you a chance to rid yourself of bitterness, anger, and self-pity today by exploring your new city, but it's up to you," she said as she began to walk away.

"Hold on a minute, I said standing up, appearing from behind my children. "I'm not bitter," I argued.

"Great, we can leave north into Freedom City," Escape replied turning around with excitement to give us a tour of Freedom City. Escape and her children wore grey jumpers with NW-D-P engraved on their backs. In the middle of Escape's rambling about how they saw the white bus the first night we arrived here, I heard Content speaking to me lowly.

"Momma, I know you don't prefer that we speak to other kids or make friends here. I know you are going to get us out of here, but for now, please let us play with Ms. Escape's kids," Content whined.

"Do you mind if my children play with your children a couple of feet away from us?" asked Escape as if she had heard Content's every word. "I don't like children in the middle of an adult conversation" Escape reasoned. Escape's kids were looking at my children eager to play. "Why don't ya'll go play a few steps down from me and your momma, my Praise is fifteen years old, and Harmony is ten, I'm sure they're around the ages of your children. Ya'll go play please, and thank you," instructed Escape as she encouraged her children to introduce themselves to mine.

All five of my children turned toward me for permission to leave their post a short distance from my watchful eyes with eagerness. "Yes, you may introduce yourselves to her children and only play several steps away from me, stay where I can see you," I commanded.

Plopping along the side of me, Escape says, "See that's better, I knew we were good friends. I always know a good friend when I see one."

"I'm not good. If I were, I wouldn't be rottening in this place talking to you. My name is Positive," I formally introduced myself to Escape.

"Everyone knows what your name is. Positive you have a call in Registration, I repeat Positive you have a call in Registration," she said with a giggle as she mimicked Lady Lost.

"Why are you bothering me? Why do you just have to befriend me? Ms. Deceitful Ways came here the same night I did, and you both wear identical jumpers, why aren't you being friendly with her?" I inquired.

"I don't like Ms. Deceitful Ways, there is something not right about her. Let me say it this way, people who make choices to live here exist in the Valley, no one makes a choice to live here on Effort Hill, and something tells me when Deceitful Ways lived in America, she made a choice to live in Effort Hill if America ever exiled her, when her kind should be in the Valley," Escape confessed as if she were entrusting me with her unfounded gossip of Ms. Deceitful Ways.

"You must really feel at home in these cells to intimately call them the Valley and Effort Hill," I said.

"I don't believe there is any intimacy involved as much as it is easier to call it the Valley or Effort Hill rather than saying 'street' each time I mention the different sections of No Where," Escape explained. "My legs begin to tingle when I sit too long, and my feet begin to hurt when I'm just standing around, so can we walk now? I know you have more questions, and I will answer them while I get some exercise, deal?" asked Escape.

"Nobody honors their deals or their word anymore, so I don't make deals. Where are we going? I asked as we walked closer to exiting No Where."

"I'm going to take you on the most wonderful tour of Freedom City and answer your questions that mystify your mind about the wonders of this place," Escape sang out with a smile. "Come on, kids, we're going on a tour through Freedom City," she announced.

"We can leave No Where and Lady Lost will not punish us, or withhold our food vouchers?" Content asked Praise walking ahead of me and Escape.

"Yes, we can leave No Where and walk around Freedom City," Escape answered Content. "Technically, the entire Freedom State is

36

No Where, and the jumpers we wear are the only thing that separates us from the Freedom City community in my opinion," Escape expressed her rational argument of our clothing representing the prison more than the people in the prison.

Still, thinking about Freedom State being No Where, I followed Escape's lead out of the prison in the same direction I saw cars exit this jail. Turning left on a street named Economy. There were different size homes and green dumpsters at the end of the block. On the corner of Effort Street and Economy Street, these dumpsters had men and women digging out of them in search of something—food, clothes, something—but why were they searching the trash? "Escape, did you see that back there?" I asked as we turned left on to Division Street from Economy Street.

"Did I see what?"

"Did you see those people wearing dingy clothes who look like they haven't taken a bath in days digging out of the dumpster and getting upset at each other over what was found?"

"Oh! Those people, we call them Castoffs. They are an alloy of veterans from the military and felons who always argue over what is left from the day," defined Escape. "Be careful around them because they can hurt you over a crumb."

"What about those cars that drive slowly through the prison?" I asked Escape who was tugging and adjusting her jumper like she needed to make a civilian's first impression to Freedom City today.

"Stay away from those cars too. They are only here to traffic drugs and alcohol to the Valley residents helping them comply with the pleas they took. I very rarely see those cars around Freedom City, so the prison must be their biggest consumers," Escape warned me, looking up from her jumper as we descended Division Street which was parallel to Effort Street. Nearing the entrance of the Valley, Escape asked the kids, "Did you notice that you can walk around No Where and completely avoid the Valley most times?"

"Yes, ma'am," they answered in unison, right before they saw a hearse next to the sidewalk in front of Registration.

"Momma, someone left No Where again," Harmony said, looking back at Escape. A casket lay between the middle of Valley Street and a parked hearse. No one seemed to care that death had visited the Valley. There wasn't one single tear trickling down anyone's face and no sounds of mourning from the onlookers. Lady Lost came out of Registration to close the rickety casket of a white jumper and officers Past loaded it onto the hearse. The driver of the hearse rolled his window down, handed Lady Lost hundreds folded into a money clip, started his ignition, and drove away. When Lady Lost glanced up from counting her money, she stared at me standing on the sidewalk across the street, and I stared at her, until Escape shoved me forward.

"What just happen?" I asked Escape with a serious tone in my voice.

"All you need to be concerned with is you and your kids being warm and mobile," Escape replied hesitant about answering my question. "You heard the phrase 'cold and stiff' that Lady Lost used repeatedly your first night here. Well, you just witnessed cold and stiff, nothing more or less to it," she said in a hurry to ramble on about something else. "Do you like the food? Did you notice we get fruit and vegetables?" Escape asked.

"Do you always talk this much about trivial things, or are you just nervous?" I asked Escape.

"I'm not the nervous type unless I'm around the cold and stiff. I just think we're going to be good friends you and me, so I may be rambling on the excitement of having a new friend," Escape responded. "A new friend, or any friend is like an unexpected gift from God, and I get overjoyed when I receive gifts from him or anyone actually. So to answer your question, Ms. Positive, I'm not nervous, that is the rhythm of my heart in my many words from the joy that I feel," continued Escape, waving her hands left and right in the air like she was directing a choir. "Positive, why do you ask so many questions and answer none?"

Ignoring Escapes question for me, I proceeded with my inquiry of No Where and surveyed Freedom City; after all, that was her deal for this little walk around we were doing. "Who is that medium-sized dark haired woman who wears the white jumper with the letters "V-I-P" written on the back?"

"There are a lot of those women in No Where, you have to be more specific," exclaimed Escape.

"This woman must be bored with the style of her jumper because she designed her jumper with a trash bag on her right leg, dirty brown torn shirts are tied around her left leg, and she wears a bowl on her head with perfect balance like she was carrying precious produce inside it. This woman also talks to herself," I added to my description of this old woman.

"Oh, that's old Ms. Sorrow, she has to be about seventy-something years old. Why you ask?" Escape walked backwards waiting on my response.

I couldn't help noticing that Ms. Sorrow talked to a lot of people around her that only she could see when she exited from the Valley at the same time the casket was being loaded. "I'm asking because that woman lives behind Registration and sneaks around like she will face punishment if Lady Lost ever catches her in sight. Escape, you didn't see her sneaking and talking to the invisible when Lady Lost was receiving her pay?" I asked.

"No, I didn't notice Ms. Sorrow leaving No Where, and no, Lady Lost knows Ms. Sorrow is an old crazy lady, who will one day become another profitable cold and stiff," answered Escape. "Everyday, Ms. Sorrow has been sneaking around the Valley before she visits the Old Library five more blocks up this street. She's been visiting the Old Library for the past five years because she tells anyone who will listen, her attorney told her to wait at the Old Library," continued Escape, "When Ms. Sorrow is at the Old Library, she always sits at the biggest square table near the window on the left side of the Old Library's entrance, waiting."

"Waiting for what?" I asked. Escape looked at me with a rude expression that I'm guessing meant my questions about Ms. Sorrow were inappropriate since I hadn't formally met the woman. Not wanting to pry further into the business of Ms. Sorrow, I changed the subject again since it seemed to be all the information I was going to gain about the people in this dreadful place.

Escape could stop giving us a tour of the city. She completed her end of the deal by confirming my judgments about No Where with her answers to my questions. The neighbors' children all have issues, from the Castoffs, Ms. Deceitful Ways, Lady Lost, a nosy Deliverance, to an old crazy woman named Sorrow, and an over-happy gray-jumper-wearing resident named Escape who has a warped mentality of prison being a happy place has affirmed my opinion about this new poverty law and No Where, we shouldn't have a membership. Besides, I couldn't handle another person's drama within Escape's false perception of this prison being fun.

Up ahead, I saw our kids having a great time becoming acquainted with each other. As we were walking I was trying to think of something else to ask Escape that might be less intrusive and break the silence. "Escape, what's those letters stand for on the backs of the residents? Why are there three different colors of jumpers?" I asked as I inhaled better, away from the polluted prison.

"When the government erased the poor from America, they required Freedom State to implement their new Poverty Residential Law based on the draft. Everyone who exists in poverty or below poverty status from the 2010 census was to be sentenced to prison for a life term. According to the new law, if a person is found guilty of poverty and your number is up in the lottery, you and your family are deported here, out of the sight and the mind of America. Some contested the draft and went to court seeking either to remain in America or a plea bargain to refrain from protesting against the draft. A plea bargain that would relieve their conscience of cowardness while in prison," Escape said her words brought back to the memory of our recent eviction from America.

She continued, "The colored jumpers with letters on the back resembles the choice a person made in court as to whether or not they would take a prosecutor's option of pleas with no contest, take their case to trial or freely surrender and report to the white bus. The yellow jumpers that your family wears reflect all the residents who refused to take a plea. "If you turn around I can tell you what your letters stand for." Escape nudged me, touching my shoulder.

"Our letters are 'NW-EH-P,'" I recited from memory to Escape without turning my back on her.

"No Where-Effort Hill-Poverty, the letters reflect where you live, what section, hill or valley, and that you're a poverty lifer for the whole Freedom City to see in case you attempt to gain employment or enroll your kids into school," Escape said as she pointed. "See these houses, gas stations, and stores we're walking by, all belong to the retired folks and disabled folks from America. "I like to think," she added, "they know our zip codes and have an idea about our credit reports by looking at our jumpers, which alerts them to protect themselves from further debt and poverty by association," as she watched the birds flying above trees with broken branches from the cold weather.

The grass was stiff when we stepped on it, as we moved out of the way of oncoming citizens walking on the sidewalk. They looked down at the ground as to not acknowledge us in their city. We proceeded forward, around the Old Library, turning right onto Independence Street with kids running and playing tag. The twins ran slower than the older children, so they decided to walk and talk to each other in their own language about the silliness of the older children as they laughed and replayed the memory of Strength tripping over Content's foot, shoving Peace into Praise, causing them to all tumble to the ground a few minutes ago with Harmony as an innocent bystander.

"Why are the retired and disabled people living in Freedom City and not in America?"

Escape responded, "My understanding is that the retired folks and disabled folks can travel between Freedom State and America. However, the trip is too expensive considering the cost of gas. So they reside in Freedom State only. The retired folks didn't plan to live so long, and their savings dwindled quickly from corporation embezzlement and stocks falling. As a result, they had to make a choice: live comfortably in Freedom City in a house and work for the rest of their years on earth, or go to court and choose which jumper to wear. As for the disabled citizens, their government funds could not compete with the economy's constant inflation, so their choice was live in Freedom City or shop at Registration for their color of jumper."

"So what does your color jumper and letters stand for?" I asked.

"My letters are 'NW-GD-P,' meaning No Where-Generational Decision, you know what the P stands for, and the gray means I'm a generational No Where resident," answered Escape.

"Are you serious? Your letters mean you've never gone to court? You wanted to live here in No Where on purpose?" I asked Escape with a confusing look on my face. Who in their right, or wrong, mind would ever want to live in a place like this? Who could be this happy to live with roaches as roommates, an allowance of food every month, medical assistance only for life and death emergency, and no education for children who live in No Where? All those additional questions I wanted to ask but dared not for fear of offending Ms. Escape's happy spirit.

"Why are you so happy to be here and act as if nothing is wrong with living in this place?" I nagged.

"Well, here is all I know, Ms. Positive, my momma lived here before she passed away, and she had me while she lived in Freedom City before she returned to No Where. And my grandma lived here before that and had raised my momma here, in No Where. It was just easier, they told me, so this place is all I know, it's home, and I'm happy to be home," replied Escape.

"It's not my home or my children's home," I said poking a hole in her joyous bubble of Freedom State patriotism.

Reading the questions on my mind from the creases in my forehead as I stared at her children, Escape answered, "Let's just say once a person is born, or an animal rather is born, in cagelike conditions, the world seems too big to matter, and the animal would prefer to remain in what they know, the cage," she assumed that satisfied my unspoken questions.

"Not a cage, but jail. No Where is a prison of poverty, not a cage, and these are not townhomes but cells with security guards who all have to be referred to as either Past, Present or Future, who also greet you early in the morning and put you outside, then return in the evening to make sure you return inside," I said passionately to Escape. "Furthermore, animals born in cages don't choose cages when a choice of living in their natural habitat is offered to them," I added.

"Girl, I think you need to breathe and chill, stop being so serious all the time and relax. I think your kids are growing gray hairs early because of your constant stressing and arguing against fate. Look, everything always has a way of working out eventually. Who knows? Maybe I remain in here because we were meant to be friends, and everyone needs a good friend in this life," she said with calmness. "Heck, maybe I'm not out of No Where because my chance is to be in No Where without the humiliation of the court, or the disappointments that come with hope and effort in America. I might be being spared of all your stress and twenty-four-hour seriousness," Escape joked.

Not getting the joke about prison, I felt my legs burn from walking, I was ready to find a seat. I had no idea Freedom City was big enough to take a long walk and not see the entire city in a day. "Momma, there is a park on Way Out Street if we make another right at this corner," pointed Strength to the sign.

"Excuse me, ladies," Peace said, "can we go to the park and eat our lunch already?" he asked with an impatient gentleman's tone.

"The park is safe for the most part, people are a bit obsessive with the rules of the park, but it's a decent place for the kids to eat," persuaded Escape.

Granting the kids permission to run to the park, I continued my conversation with Escape.

"Why do the Valley residents have to go outside at the same time in the morning as the rest of us, but they have no curfew at night?" I asked

"Finally, an easy question to answer," Escape celebrated approaching a picnic table in the park. The Valley residents who took a plea are the ones who don't have an evening curfew as per the conditions of their plea. An early morning rise and outside call are their only rules, otherwise they would be unable to comply with the different pleas they accepted."

"What does a curfew have to do with complying with a plea," I asked confused. "You keep implying that the Valley residents need help with their pleas, like the drug dealers in the cars, and no curfew. What pleas can an inmate accept that they need help to serve in prison?"

"Give it time. You will figure out some of the answers to your questions on your own," replied Escape, changing the subject. "What did you bring for lunch? We brought ham sandwiches."

"We brought peanut butter and jelly sandwiches with some fruit," I stated, thinking back on the sounds of our first night in prison. There were ambulances and screams of horror coming from the Valley, and that's all part of the Valley plea? Glad I didn't accept Supercilious's pleas. My thoughts are everywhere, unable to settle down in my mind from all the information it has received about this place. I'm beginning to get a headache, and I'm too curious to stop asking Escape questions.

I was staring at Escape eating her sandwich in bewilderment as to why she would choose to reside in No Where and not take a chance to survive in America. I returned to the subject of assigned jumpers, asking if my acronym of Ms. Sorrow's jumper was accurate. "Ms. Sorrow's jumper read "V-I-P" so she lives in the Valley, she took some sort of plea, and she's a fellow lifer of poverty, is that right?" I questioned Escape.

"You got it. You're a fast learner, now may I finish my lunch with the kids and take a break from adult conversation?" Escape asked me in between swallows. My stomach growled in agreement.

5

I didn't want to end Positive's questioning of me. I just wanted to step back from her and her children's determination to not belong to No Where even though they were already members. Positive's motivation and determination makes me think that my parenting is somehow insufficient, like I should have taught my children to be more than content with wherever they found themselves in life. My parents weren't content with anything they had in life, so I made sure learning to be content was a priority that I felt my children needed.

But now I see, maybe, I should have taught them to always want more than their circumstances. I don't know, perfect parenting didn't come with a manual, I thought as I considered my past. When I watch Positive's attitude about this place and how she has her children's strict obedience, I marvel at her obvious efforts that she had to make to prevent her children from living in No Where—and all her efforts failed. That is exactly what I'm afraid of the most, failing. There are too many negative what-if questions that could happen to us in America, and we could still end up in prison. What is the point of leaving prison? To do a full circle over the course of years to wind up in prison again? I wish I could just leave and take a chance, have an adventure in America even if it turned out wrong, but now wrong is No Where; since I'm already here, why should I leave?

I know when Positive speaks to me in a rude manner that her rudeness stems from the root of disappointment in herself to provide her family with more than the conditions of No Where. It is this unquiet determination for survival embedded in her soul that drew my friendship close. I am amazed at her unsettled heart to make prison their home. People like Positive are destined to leave No Where either by an amended law or sure self-will even if she does walk in a dream of defeat for the moment. She is a fast learner and well educated because she remembers everything a person says when they say it like a lawyer, and I can't remember her children's names.

Positive is sharp tongued and very irritated that she ended up nowhere surrounded by us failed residents who claim there is no way out. She'll get out of here though, I know she will even if she doesn't believe in herself anymore. I may not be educated, but I do know things, and I know Positive will be free when she releases the negative thoughts in her mind that come with a life sentence term in No Where.

That is where we are drastically different people because I don't have negative thoughts about this prison in my mind. I live in No Where and it doesn't bother me. I have no ambition to leave No Where, and I probably never will. My grandmother, Maya, was born somewhere in Europe and lived in St. Petersburg, Russia. Ousted by her father for choosing an American to marry, she came to America in the early 1930s. My American grandfather moved her here to America from Tver City when she gave birth to my mom, Liliya, in Virginia. My grandfather didn't want any children before he became rich. He wasn't prepared for a family, so he deserted grandma Maya and my mom when she was an infant. Grandma Maya spoke very little English and made bad choices in men to take care of them. Consequently, No Where had become her state of mind before this place ever existed.

My grandmother raised my mom in ghettos with roaches, ants in the summer, cold water, and no electricity. Sometimes my mother would tell me about her childhood poverty conditions, but she seemed happy when I would listen to her stories about sharing the poor life with Grandma Maya. When the poverty system became enforced in 1978, Grandma Maya was so thrilled to relocate to a better building that she and one landlord took their own plea, celebrated with a bottle of vodka. My mom said the vodka changed from a celebration to depression when she no longer concerned herself with suitable housing for mom because welfare was better than any ghetto in Europe. Grandma Maya began to hear those negative thoughts replay in her mind about grandpa deserting her and marrying someone else and beginning a family after their dreams to have a family and lots of children—only to lose her husband over the untimely birth of mom. Grandma Maya swore to never love again and resided in the valley of her bottle while raising mom.

Eventually, my Mom grew up and moved out of Grandma's mental prison of vodka into the confinement of my dad's wanton promises. Pretend was my dad's name, and he made my mom look and feel like a queen every day of the week of every year and never married her. He said he needed to save money for the biggest ring that reminded her of his love for the rest of her life. My mom would have settled for a simple gold band, but he had to give her more as if caring for my mom was his ultimate accomplishment in life. My dad ran a business that he explained was profitable without being illegal. He exploited women who had No Where frames of mind in America like Grandma Maya. They didn't care about being misused, and my dad was just the person to care about profiting off their self-devalue. Pretend purchased a four-bedroom house in which he used two bedrooms for business in Maryland. Business was great, and my mom had everything he wanted to give her, everything except the marriage she desired.

Six years after the fiscal bliss of the prostitution business, I was born on my mom's favorite holiday, New Year's Eve, where each tomorrow you get a new year and new choices to begin to make your life better, she always said. My mom named me Escape, because she wanted me to experience all the wonders of life that surpassed the limited desire of relationships with men. We lived in a ghetto-hood in Baltimore, Maryland, around Eager Street When I was becoming of age to be considered a lady, my mom always said there was nothing my dad wouldn't give me.

One night a man came into the house when my father was gone and my mother was asleep. I tried to tell him that the ladies would be here at night, and my father was on his way home, but he wouldn't listen. He put his hands over my mouth and walked me into one of the business rooms. Slamming me on the bed, he placed a knife against my face, threatening to cut my head off if I woke my mother up while he ripped my pajama pants off of me. I tried to scream no and push him off of me as hard as I could, but nothing worked.

The palm of his hand was bigger than my face; I felt smothered. Lying there with tears of no streaming down my face and weakly touching his hand that covered my mouth, I heard the screen door close, and my dad announce that he was home.

This strange man whispered, "Nothing's gonna happen to me because I'm a veteran of the military and stronger than your dad. Be quiet or I'll kill you." He demanded that I be still and stop squirming as he permitted his knife to kiss my face, leaving blood trickling down around my eye. I could barely see with tears and blood entering my eye as I tried to yell, "Dad". I was in the business room hearing him calling my name, but the man was stronger than me.

Eventually, my dad came into the room with a block of wood swinging at this man, hitting him in the mouth as he tried to explain why he was on top of me with his pants down. There was so much noise. My mom woke up and took me out of the room with no questions. My dad continued to beat this stranger to death, and I wanted my dad to kill him. I don't know how long my dad beat the stranger because my mom closed the door behind us, and we never came back.

Later that night, the police arrived to our home and arrested my dad for the death of the stranger, the enemy of women. My parents argued over the phone daily, my dad wanted my mother to bail him out of jail, and my mother wanted her new rules for our family to be understood. Mom wanted nothing to do with my dad's business after what happened to me, so she constantly turned the business women away when they would knock at the door reporting for work. She spent all the savings on the bills, my dad's bailout, and my dad's attorney until poverty visited again.

Neither of them ever asked me how I was doing; they just kept telling me I would be okay every day as my stomach grew and I gave birth to Praise. Praise was five years old before my dad began to enjoy being a grandfather and I began to acknowledge him as my son.

Praise stayed with my parents most of the time, and I dated a new man every night just like the business until Harmony would greet the world in nine months. Being pregnant again and not knowing who the father was became a huge argument between my parents. One minute they would yell at each other over Harmony, and the next, my mom would yell that my dad's business and addiction to compliments of how well he was providing for his family is what ruined me, before she would slam their bedroom door that would never close completely. Through the crack of the door, I could see mom lying across the bed with the pillows supporting her head and tears running from her eyes, repeating the words, "my Escape needs to slow down".

Of course, I slowed down after Harmony and learned to celebrate my children even when I see the stranger in the face of Praise. Learning to be the best mother to my children that my mom was to me, I kept a janitorial job, cleaning grade schools during the week, and I folded laundry for housekeeping in the nursing homes. Everything wasn't great, but we survived, until management discovered I had no high school diploma and fired me after ten years of employment with them. It seemed like we went from poverty to below the line of poverty in a weekend.

My mother was glad when No Where came into existence a few years before the draft because she had enough of America's dreams of wealth that only lasted my childhood and mid-adolescent years. My mom and dad moved all of us to the decision area of No Where, wearing grey jumpers because they volunteered to live here before it became a law, they weren't drafted. Lady Lost explained that we could live in Effort Hill until our numbers came up or we could have a second chance at living in America before poverty became illegal.

One day, we came home from this park, the same one we're having lunch in with Positive right now, to find my dad wearing a white jumper with letters "V-S-P," cold and stiff in the bathtub hours after he said he was going to court to discuss alternatives to poverty with the prosecutor. He had voluntarily took a plea of suicide. I guess the failure of providing for us was greater than his love of being with us. Soon after the hearse drove off with my dad, grief overtook my mom's mind, and she had a hard time remembering who I was or why I was in her townhome most days. So Lady Lost went to court and had my mom committed to the Valley on the basis of insanity for a profit.

On the first night in the Valley with my mom, Lady Lost visited to tell me one day we're all going to be cold and stiff. We wore white jumpers with the letters "V-I-P" as long as my mother was alive. Later that week before my mom died she told me what my name meant to her. She said it was my written proof and authority to escape nowhere thoughts of negativity and this government system of No Where. She explained that No Where is not a ghetto in the capacity that my ancestors suffered in; there were no freight cars and there were no massacred people because of a religious preference here, so I was free to escape. She said in America you still have electricity, plumbing, windows, and central heating. This prison is an escapable place. The only thing she didn't tell me was how to escape. Kissing her grandchildren and telling them to laugh all the time, she passed away holding my hand.

After she passed away, I took Lady Lost's opportunity to reside in No Where until I made a decision, and we returned to the gray jumpers. As an adult, I dated someone retired and of no importance to me now. He lived here and I have no desire to chase America's dream of success only to find myself on a rollercoaster of disappointments, which will inevitably cause me to return to poverty. Instead of riding delusional rollercoasters of wealth, I decided to teach my family how to make the most of living in poverty by showing them how to be content with priceless possessions, using our fun memories and my humming peaceful melodies to them every night while they slept. I named my children after the music that hummed in my soul through the hard times of my life when I would imagine myself dancing to escape the hurt.

I am determined to make each day a day of escape for my children as we meet interesting people or discover something different about Freedom City. No day will ever be the same for them like the designs of heaven are never the same with each morning we wake up. My kids are experiencing a different day right now as we have the honor to eat with a friend whose name is famous in No Where within the first week, and she doesn't know any of us.

I sit here watching Ms. Positive have lunch with her kids, and I know she is only visiting No Where until she can escape her defeating thoughts of failure.

6

"It's time to leave before we're late for curfew. Throw away the trash from our sandwiches while I wipe the twins' hands and faces," I announced to my children who were sitting close to Praise and Harmony like they were estranged cousins reunited.

"Is your mom always this uptight?" asked Praise.

"Yeah, she acts like a drill sergeant," added Harmony in agreement to her brother's question as they walked to the sidewalk to wait for Ms. Positive and her Mom on the sidewalk.

"That's our mom you're talking about, and if you don't like the way she is, then you don't like us," Peace stated with a matter of fact attitude directed to Praise.

"I need you to relax Peace, I think you're as uptight as your mom. You must be her favorite since you tend to stress before you rest. No one said we didn't like your mom," corrected Praise.

"My brother isn't uptight, and neither is our mom," interrupted Strength. "She doesn't want us to get comfortable with living below our potential. She wants us to be prosperous and tells us our destiny is to become educated and trained in the career of our choice. Our mom is unlike your mom, who seems to let you two live loosely with no principles or desires to do better for yourselves." Strength lectured as she finished discarding the trash from their meal and joined Praise, Harmony, and Peace on the sidewalk waiting to be escorted to the cell.

"Why are you guys so upset all the time, am I permitted to speak freely about what I notice about a person, or do you have rules for what is acceptable for me to say?" asked Praise.

"You can say whatever you like, just don't say nothing about our mom," Content responded as she too joined them on the sidewalk holding the twins' hands.

"Don't talk about Mommy," Truth and Reason agreed in unison whose attention to this conversation was soon changed by their observance of ants walking in a line toward food on the ground. The twins stood looking at the ground with the residue of a frown left on their faces.

"What's the matter Truth and Reason?" I asked. From the sound of the twins, all of the kids were saying something about me.

"Don't get in that, kids have disagreements all the time, let them figure it out on their own," suggested Escape.

Did Escape just give me parenting instructions? I thought as I now began to have creases and groves in my forehead. I can see her friendship with me will soon be terminated because I don't coparent my children with strangers. Especially strangers who believe they have succeeded in failing to try at life. Ignoring Escape's comment, I asked again if there was something wrong, but all the children including Praise and Harmony remained quiet.

Walking west on Independence Street, I saw Ms. Sorrow leaving the Old Library in a hurry toward the Valley.

"Are we late?" I asked Escape.

"No, we will make it back before curfew," Escape responded. "I told you to stop studying Ms. Sorrow. She is crazy, and you will be crazy too if you don't learn to ignore that woman," Escape repeated while laughing at my nervousness to return to Effort Hill. Turning left onto Division Street, I decided to walk my children up the hill and around to our cell, avoiding the Valley. I have enough sad thoughts in my mind to last me a lifetime; my children don't need to see and implant the Valley's sadness for a lifetime memory.

"Are you going to start avoiding the Valley and walk the long way around when you leave Effort Hill from now on?" asked Escape as we walked by the Valley.

"Mom, maybe we need to walk through the Valley because you have to get your injection," Content reminded me with a low voice that could still be heard by Escape's nosy ears.

"What injection?" inquired Escape. "Positive, are you sick?" she asked looking at me with sympathy and pity. It is that look of weakness in Escape's face that I despise the most. I don't want anyone feeling sorry for me, not even strangers.

"None of your business," I answered Escape. "My personal life isn't your concern." I said glaring at Content for being heard.

"Momma, are you going to get it?" Content asked. "It's too late, she knows now."

"She doesn't know anything, and yes I'm going to get it. I'll get it after you all are safely in front of the cell," I responded to Content while ignoring Escape's attempts to be noticed and heard.

"Excuse me, I'm here, and I'm not going home yet, so is anyone going to tell me what we're not talking about here?" asked Escape.

"No," I responded turning my attention toward Escape. "Feel free to walk through the Valley if you like, but my children and I will walk around from now on."

"A simple yes would have sufficed," said Escape. "So you're not going to share your illness with me?" Escape's nosiness persisted while walking west on Economy Street. My children and I ignored Escape's question as we watched the Castoffs ending their day of scuffles with each other, sleeping in boxes and using some type of torn material as a blanket for an evening rest. Finally, turning South on Effort Street, we made it to our cells with 20 minutes to spare. My children were so exhausted that no one spoke a word not even to bid Ms. Escape, Praise, or Harmony a good night. As Escape descended from cell #C walking backwards, she yelled, "You may ignore my question about your illness for now, but it will get answered" before yawning as she turned to walk home.

"Peace and Strength, watch the twins for me. Content and I are going to the Valley to retrieve my injection," I instructed giving the twins to their siblings and snatching Content's hand, walking with a fast pace to Registration.

"You need to get your injection a lot sooner if you don't want any problems with Lady Lost and inside call," Deliverance advised handing me the injection when I opened the door.

"Thank you," I said, receiving the injection and walking toward the exit of Registration.

"I'm glad you're here," said Lady Lost. "Your attorney called while you were gone exploring Freedom City with Escape today. I don't like attorneys, they are bad for business. Next time, be around to answer his call, hear?" asked Lady Lost rhetorically.

Before I could respond, Deliverance complemented Lady Lost on her skirt and blouse, while he pointed to his watch reminding me of the short time I had before inside call. Content and I left Registration running uphill and walking past officers Future. I grabbed my sleeping twins from Peace and Strength and waited for Content to open the door. Managing to turn around with arms full of kids, I was trying to see what the officers did when we were on our way inside. All they do is turn east and face the streets like stone statues. I could have worked a job like that and supported my family just fine, I thought, and then I stepped inside for the night.

* * *

For the past few months, my children and I have lived in No Where being nothing and thinking about nothing worth any value. Mr. Grace has continually attempted to contact me, and I have avoided every phone call. My children walk to the park for exercise daily, and I don't see Escape often; but when I do, she nods her head toward me in approval of my family leaving No where every day. Although, I didn't feel much like leaving No Where when I woke up at 4:00 a.m. this morning on the center of the floor in the cold living room listening to the officers complete their routine of knocking and yelling "Wake up!" Today, I just want sit in front of the cell, in front of the sunlight that seems to be confused about the seasons every day in this state. Now that I think about it, there hasn't been a cloudy day since we arrived in No Where, and I sure wish there was one today.

"Good morning," greeted Lady Lost. "You know it's about that time, is everyone ready to come out of there yet?" she inquired as she tried to peek through the window of the cell.

"Not yet, we have until 6 a.m. before we have to come outside, we'll be outside on time," I yelled through the window. The kids scrambled to put their jumpers on faster because they heard Lady Lost's voice.

"Momma, what are we going to do today that we haven't done every day?" asked Peace. "Every day we take a walk to the park, eat, and come back to the cell. I miss going to school," Peace stated while he was putting on his shoes, leaving us to stare at him in amazement. This was the first time we ever heard Peace protest for not attending school, and the first time we heard him hint that he liked school. "Why is everybody staring at me?" Peace asked.

"No reason," I said. "We are going to the Old Library today, and you all are going to read. I can't take you to school because you're forbidden to be around Freedom City school kids, but that doesn't mean you have to be anyone's dummy. Those old books are just as good as the new books and better than technology, considering I'm raising you to think, not to input data into you brains meaninglessly like a machine," I lectured all of them for the millionth time about books being better than computers as they descended the stairs in birth order, Content and Strength dreading a day of learning with each exaggerated step toward the door.

Stepping outside, I could see a mourning dove sitting on a tree branch and a hermit thrush on the icy ground eating berries and other birds flying above the naked trees into sunlit clouds. It is very cold today, I thought, watching the officers divide themselves in groups with additional officers to again knock on the doors of those who refused to come outside. Officers Past and their group were in the Valley yelling, "Open the door and get out, or we coming in to put you out!"

Officer Future and his group stood in the middle of the street watching the residents make the decision to come outside slowly before they had to reinforce the outside rule with their keys and a visit to Lady Lost. All of the residents seemed to move with a sluggish motion as they groaned their way into the morning light. Something must have happened last night that caused the residents to walk with weights of despair on their ankles, but I don't want to know about it. I'm just grateful it didn't happen in cell C.

"You had another phone call in Registration early this morning, it was your lawyer again," complained Lady Lost.

"If I haven't come to answer the phone, then I wasn't available clearly," I said from in front of #C.

"Look, I'm not your secretary, and I don't like talking to any lawyers, so the next time he calls either you answer or I will reduce your food allowance," demanded Lady Lost while she wiped her high heels with a Kleenex before littering the earth.

"Good morning ya'll, what a beautiful day to be outside," Escape said as she approached #C trying to defuse a potential feud between me and Lady Lost that she heard in the tone of our voices from three townhomes down. "My kids and I have nothing planned as usual every day, so I was wondering if we could join ya'll in doing nothing?" she asked watching me stare at Lady Lost and Lady Lost stare at me.

"Yes, that would be great, Ms. Escape, if you and your clan join this clan doing nothing and being nothing today. While you spend time with your friend here, remind her that I'm the keeper here in No Where and not her co-inmate," Lady Lost said to Escape, never taking her eyes off of me. "I don't like to be upset, so explain to her what happens if I should feel upset by her," she added walking away in the direction of Registration.

"You don't have to explain anything to me," I howled to Escape loud enough for Lady Lost and Effort Hill to hear. "Keeper or not, Lady Lost doesn't intimidate me. She has one phone to receive incoming calls, so receive them."

"Hey, do you know where you are?" asked Escape with so much stress and tension in her shoulders, they appeared to reach her ears, "Lady Lost will starve you and your children for long periods of time, so long that your kids will make a request to be cold and stiff. Trust me, you don't want to make your stay here a difficult one. Do whatever Lady Lost wants and make your stay here as pleasant as possible for the sake of your children if for no other reason," Escape pleaded.

"Are you done following Lady Lost's instructions?" I asked, noticing Deceitful Ways standing on her step focusing her attention in our direction while recording everything she heard, unlike the other residents who walked away after Lady Lost left my cell. "Why are you here and what do you want on this beautiful day?" mocking Escape with an attitude, I picked up my twins preparing to leave No Where.

"My kids and I thought we could do nothing with you and your children today. Is that okay?" requested Escape.

"We are not doing nothing today, I'm taking my loves to the Old Library. They have been without school long enough. It's time for them to read something. Who knows? Maybe, I will find a book also and escape from this prison," I stated sarcastically.

"Okay, then we will join you at the Old Library. It's about time I let the kids see the importance of being educated. What do you think? More importantly, what did Lady Lost want with you early in the morning? She hates being outside in the morning," Escape returned our conversation back to the incident that transpired before she approached my cell.

"My attorney, Grace, called me again. I don't want to hear 'be patient and wait for me to fix your situation,' so I don't answer his calls. We have been here for three months, and he hasn't fixed anything yet." I said. "Lady Lost doesn't like speaking to attorneys and wants me to take his calls so his constant calling will be minimized."

"How do you know he hasn't fixed anything if you won't answer any of his calls?" asked Escape.

"It doesn't take a philosopher to think on the possibility that Grace has fixed our situation if we still live here. Are you always this smart, or is that attributed to your being nothing?" I asked.

"You had better be glad it's a beautiful day today because I might have taken offense to what you just said," argued Escape. "Have you done what Grace advised and waited on him to fix your situation, or have you walked around in defeated silence, bitter that you're here talking to me almost every day?" asked Escape.

"I have nothing else to do but wait, wait, wait, and wait until Lady Lost makes her profit off of us. Don't you see me waiting?" I asked. "I am waiting for something to happen, or for life to divorce me, but I'm waiting, that's all I do every day is wait."

"Momma, Ms. Escape's kids are coming across the street to join us. So do you mind if we walk ahead of you and hangout with Ms. Escape's kids?" Content interrupted my waiting sermon to Escape, clearly avoiding an adult conversation.

"Fine, Content, but do not lose sight of your siblings on our way to the Old Library, at the Old Library, or on our way home," I instructed putting the twins on the ground so they could run catching up to the older kids.

"Maybe you should answer the calls. What if the verdict was reversed, or he knows some other way of getting you out? You will never know what he wants until you take the call," persisted Escape, refusing to change the subject.

"Maybe I should, maybe I shouldn't. I answered a lot of his calls through pretrial and trial, and they all came to no avail, so maybe I shouldn't," I replied.

"Everyone knows you don't want No Where to be your home," said Escape before changing her thought toward the kids. "Kids, hold on a minute, don't walk north leaving from Effort Hill when you are just going to have to walk around the block and come down hill passing the Valley on Division Road. Today, we're taking the simple route through the Valley, and making a left onto Division Road toward the Old Library, it's faster. It's always good to change your route a bit in case someone is watching you. No one wants to be a victim," suggested Escape.

"Momma said we can't ever, ever, never ever walk through No Where after the first time you walked us around No Where," Truth informed Miss Escape. "She said you hang around gloom and you'll become gloomy," Truth said in unison with Reason.

Escape kept her eyes staring into mine for approval as she said, "Well, Truth, ya'll getting ready to walk through the Valley today, it's about time you saw the whole No Where intimately for your own safety, if for nothing else. I mean, if someone was chasing you or one of these questionable residents tried to hurt you, shouldn't you know many directions to maneuver around No Where and Freedom City for safety?" asked Escape.

Escape did make a good argument. If someone ever tried to hurt my children, they would need many ways and hideouts to avoid becoming a stranger's victim. As much as I did not like strangers and I did not want to make friends here, maybe Escape isn't such a bad person. Her conversation does make the time tick away faster; besides my kids could use a few permanent friends, and I could use all of Escape's knowledge about this place in order to teach my children who not to become as adults.

I conceded to Escape's suggestion, "Listen to Ms. Escape today, only for today," giving my children the permission they were seeking to travel into the Valley again. "Pay close attention to Truth and Reason when crossing the streets," I lectured as my children remained in front of me while Praise and Harmony urged them to join their desire to run down the hill.

My children's faces looked puzzled as they remained standing before me like I didn't give them permission to go. This was the first time they ever saw me let anyone change my mind to my rules, or have anyone tell my kids what to do and I followed their suggestion. Today was unlike any day they had ever experienced since we arrived to No Where; today became a day of fun. They ran screaming with laughter down the hill.

The residents were barely greeting Escape for staring at me in awe that my family ran downhill laughing, and I was walking through No Where in no rush for the first time. The ground had a blanket of grass patches that surrounded most cells as we neared the middle of the Valley. Leaves on the trees began to unlock their different shades of green as they caught the reflection of the light that accompanied our new path toward the Old Library. I noticed a shadowy presence of hopeless gloom covering the townhomes in the Valley, as many residents attempted to hide their faces avoiding Escape's acknowledgements.

"Hold on a minute, Escape," I interrupted her tour of pointing out residents and sharing their family histories so I could quickly get the attention of my children in the distance that seemed to be growing larger by the pace of their walk.

"Mis amores, se quedan mas cerca de mi donde yo puedo ver, por favor," I got my children's attention before they crossed the Division Road.

"Sí, Mami," they replied in unison.

"Mami, Después de cruzar la calle de la nada, nos detendremos en cada esquina y esperar para usted, vale?" asked Peace.

"Whoa, what just happened here? You didn't tell me you spoke another language. What did you say to your kids in Spanish, and what did they say to you? Don't leave anything out," pleaded Escape for a translation.

"I will tell you what was said this one time, but please don't ask me again because the answer will be no," I stated to Escape, feeling embarrassed that she was making a big deal out my being bilingual. "I told my loves to stay closer to me where I could see them. They replied, 'Yes, Mom.' Then Peace informed me that after they cross the street from No Where, they will stop at every corner and wait for me."

Looking at Escape's amazement like she was suddenly transported to a Hispanic country, I asked, "How did you know the language we spoke was Spanish?"

"Really, did you just ask me that? Look around you, whether you're in No Where or a citizen in America, there are a lot of Hispanics nowadays who live among us, what other language could it have been?" Escape asked rhetorically.

"Are you this dramatic and full of energy for every question you answer?"

"Um, let me see, I have to think intelligently about this, yep," teased Escape.

"Hey, you didn't answer my other question?"

"What other question, you ask a lot of questions?" I said.

"No more than you now, how did you learn Spanish?" inquired Escape.

Keeping an eye on my children, I think I saw Ms. Sorrow enter the Old Library. "I would rather not talk about myself if you don't mind, my memories are just that, memories, and they should all be left in the past so I don't trip and fall over them trying to walk forward," I replied to Escape almost out of breath from walking up the stairs to the Old Library.

"We have finally reached this Old Library. Let's go, kids, something different to do and learn because we finally have different, good friends to do it with," cheered Escape pouring her excitement into the hearts of the kids.

7

"I will never get used to those twenty-five steps outside before I reach the door of this place," I said as air tried to knock on the door of my lungs for permission to enter.

"You shouldn't be that out of shape, Positive, I see you walking around the city with the kids daily," said Escape with a laugh as we entered the library.

A brown carpet was extended from the entrance, past the reception desk, and downstairs to the youth area of the Old Library. It had high ceilings and books on shelves that appeared to be waiting for someone to choose them for a formal dance in their mind like they were at a royal ball of knowledge. Large and small study tables with many lamps stood in rows of two in a center space in front of the shelves lonely and deserted by scholars. Whispering to my children to walk while they raced their way to the youth area, I heard a faint sound coming from this enormously wide study table near the right side of the entrance.

"Did you hear that?" I asked Escape.

"Hear what?"

"Psst, psst, psssst!"

That sound is coming from the left, and Escape is ignoring that clear sound aimed to get our attention.

"I'm not looking for sounds, I'm going to play with the kids. Didn't you say we were learning today, and you were teaching?" asked Escape. "I'm focusing on my lesson, not sounds, and you should too," she said.

"Yes, I am going to teach today, but my children are here to focus on reading primarily," I said. "I am certain Ms. Sorrow's sound is trying to get my attention, so could you do me a favor and tell my children I'll join them in an hour, please," I asked Escape as I walked to the left of the entrance toward Ms. Sorrow's table and noticed her beginning to panic with each step I took closing the distance between myself and her seat.

"No problem, you can get distracted by the crazy if you want to friend, just remember that I warned you the lady is crazy," replied Escape before exiting the first floor of the library downstairs to the youth area.

"Stop where you are, and don't you dare sit in that seat, or you'll have to deal with me," instructed Ms. Sorrow, greeting me with a warning.

Ms. Sorrow is sitting at a huge table alone, and she has assigned seating. Yes, okay, assigned seats at an empty table makes me agree with Escape. Ms. Sorrow is crazy. "May I sit with you, Ms. Sorrow, I couldn't help but notice that the sound *pssst* was coming from this direction. Was that you calling me? Do you need help with something?" I questioned standing four steps from her and the table.

"I don't know what you're talking about, there were no sounds coming from this direction," groaned Ms. Sorrow. "I was busy talking with my kids until you came over here bothering us," said Ms. Sorrow as she rose from her chair, walking and looking around the table ensuring all the chairs were comfortable.

"You either have something to say to me or you don't, it doesn't matter to me. If you were not trying to get my attention, I will leave you in peace and return to my own living children," I said, my eyes piercing straight through to her eyes when she returned to her seat. *My time is precious when my children have to wait on me, so either she is going to talk or I am going to leave*, I thought.

"That's just the problem, I don't know if my children are alive or dead anymore. I don't even know if I'm a grandmother. Please, grab a chair from that table over there and join us," she said, pointing diagonally to an empty table across from her table.

I cannot believe I'm dragging an additional chair to the table when there are four empty chairs at this one. I sat down a chair away from her so we could have a square table of reasoning. I asked, "How can I be of service to you, Ms. Sorrow?" hoping that I was talking to the part of her that realized she was talking to me.

"For right now, just sit down and listen. I watched you when you first arrived to the prison. You came in through the Valley, two cell rows from my townhome, and Lady Lost put you and your kids in cell C on Effort Hill." With interest piqued, I listened intently to Ms. Sorrow because she too agreed with me: No Where is a prison, a prison of poverty, and those townhomes are nothing more than cells enclosed by the bars of security guards.

"Don't look so shocked that I noticed your family. I notice all the families that enter into No Where by the hundreds and exit No Where in smaller cells of cold stillness. My observation of your family is not what I want with you. I am not interested in gossiping to you about everything I've seen over the six years that I've been here. You, Positive, are someone who will remember me and my children sitting here in the Old Library, which is why I called you over here," she continued as she glanced over the empty chairs.

"My time is expiring and we want someone to remember us and our journey in America in case one day I become cold and still. I don't want our existence to become insignificant to the world when someone in the heavens thought enough of us to create us among all the other citizens of America," she said as her eyes penetrated through my eyes to my mind's storage of memory files.

"What is it that you want me to remember?" I asked impatiently. Since Ms. Sorrow believed herself to be unimportant to America, what difference would it make if I remembered who she and her family were when America rejected me too?

"Can you just sit there and listen. If I want you to speak or ask me a question—I already know you're going to ask—I will tap the table softly as to not disturb Henry across from me sleeping. Henry loves to sleep in this Old Library's solitude." She tapped on the table.

"I understand, I will speak only when I hear your tap," I said not wanting to upset a crazy woman and never taking my eyes off her hunched posture as she leaned toward me, beginning to share my breathing space with every word she spoke.

"I knew you would understand me, I knew you were smart. My medications the Life and Death Hospital gave me only allow me about ten minutes of focus at a time to speak with anyone before my mind returns from its vacation to paralyzing depression from the death of my husband, and lingering hurt from the theft of my children. Before I begin, I mustn't be rude." Pointing at each chair she introduced me, "These are my four children: Henry, Henrietta, Hope, and Happy, meet smart girl,".

I turned and looked at the four chairs and turned back to Ms. Sorrow.

"It's rude to not say hi to my children when hi never killed anybody," said Ms. Sorrow with a disgusted look on her face for my lack of manners to the invisible. She tapped the table.

"I apologize. Hi, children," I said in utter disbelief that I was speaking to human chairs.

"Each one of my children that sit here before you used to be visible to your preference of how you see people until I was robbed of them. Hell, they used to be visibly living with me as I worked three jobs to support us before that new law passed about a poverty system or something. My children and I were doing just fine, weren't we, children?"

Ms. Sorrow, now looking at her chairs, breathed slowly and deeply before she continued, "My Love used to be a car assembler in America. When the heavens separated us, he left me with a nice handsome retirement. His retirement alone would not support us in America, so I thought it was a blessing when the poverty system came into existence. If we could live in a place that cost less and financially survive, I thought why not live in Freedom State. So my children and I moved into Freedom City just on the other side of Independence Street, near the park." Her eyes were beginning to fill with water.

"I worked from 11 p.m. to 7 a.m. at the same factory our food allowances come from when we first moved here. I was a janitor at the factory, and I made $5 an hour. I returned home by 8 a.m., and Henry would have all the kids ready for school eating breakfast at the table, just like his father, my late husband, used to do before he passed away beside me when the sun rose September 24, 2013.

"At 10 a.m. I would leave home in a hurry to reach my library job at this very library as a book stocker for $4.40 an hour until 3 p.m. Then I would rush home again take a two-hour nap and begin my waitressing job at 7 p.m. halfway across the city at Quitters Club until 10:00 p.m. for $2.50 an hour plus tips, before I would have to return to the factory. I didn't mind the not sleeping because I was determined to keep my children out of the new No Where prison the government decided to build in this state." She tapped on the table while tears escaped her eyes and cascaded down her cheeks.

"Why were you working so many jobs when you had your late husband's handsome retirement money, isn't Freedom City supposed to be economically stable for the retired?" I asked on cue waiting for her answer.

Ms. Sorrow began to talk to her children like I was no longer in the room. She asked Happy if he had done everything his teacher asked him to do because she didn't want any bad reports given to Love that they would have to discuss when she returned home. Then in a second's time she remembered I was waiting on an answer and continued her conversation with me.

"Love's retirement only supported the food and mortgage here. We still needed utilities, medical, dental, monthly toiletries, and clothing. Taxes and medical insurance rules have not changed for the residents of Freedom City just because we live outside of America. The Life and Death Hospital is the only medical facility here, and I could not afford their services for three years because they complied with the government's No Mercy Medical Care Act in 2012. I'm not real educated, so I'll do my best to explain this act. It meant the first year my children and I went uninsured, I would have to pay $95 to the government for each member of my family for twelve months, which came to $5,700. If we went uninsured for a second year, I would have to pay $325 for each member of my family, which came to $19,500. Then, if I was unable to afford medical insurance for the third year, I would have to pay $555 for each member of my family, which came to $33,300. So I have been working many jobs to pay the debt of our inability to afford medical insurance. When the retirement money dwindled to nothing from the purchase of the house and our home expenses, I had no choice but to work. The pay isn't that great in America or here, so I worked three jobs every hour the clocked ticked," she continued speaking, now staring out of the window.

"When Love and I worked, life was good. He worked most of the hours, and I worked part time in the library, while raising our kids in America. I read a lot and I was the smarter between the both of us from listening to people's conversations and looking over their shoulder at the words on paper as they read aloud to whoever was in their company. We had plans to put me through school and become a power couple one day," she said with a chuckle, "until he died, leaving Henry, my nine-year-old, to look after his brother and sisters while I worked triple time for three years," she tapped the table.

"Where are your children, your visible children now?" I asked sitting forward in my chair feeling the suspense of Ms. Sorrow's testimony.

"Hope, stop being so mean, let your brother rest his head on your shoulder. Who cares if he drools a little bit? A little brotherly sweetness won't hurt you a bit," she said to the second chair before answering me. "This new poverty system is very different than the one they used when my mother was alive. It used to be a parent had sole rights and authority over their children to make them productive, law-abiding citizens in America. Now the children have rights to tell the parents what laws are current that give them the freedom of disobedience and rudeness in the home, at school, and to any authority figures until they reach a legal adult age to be sent to state or federal prisons.

"DCFS, Department of Children and Family Services has become DPCFS, Dismissing Parents from their Children Forever System in Freedom State. This system has rules about how to take care of your children according to the government's approval, and if you did not comply with their list of rules, then they took your kids." She tapped on the table.

"Why did the government dismiss your parental rights, and where are your children?" I asked intently.

"Henrietta and Hope, make sure you mind your brother while I'm gone. We need this money to keep our house and pay the bills. The last thing I need is for something to happen to any of you, so do like I say and mind Henry, you hear?" demanded Sorrow of the chairs before answering my question.

"The government just took my kids one day. I didn't know they were going to be taken and the caseworker reminded me that we did not have a phone when I appeared in court. So, the DCPFS people took my children at some point when I was away from home October 5, 2016, on Henry's sixteenth birthday. I tried to explain to the courts and the DCPFS people that I worked three jobs so I could support my kids without government assistance. I begged them to see that I was making every effort to not be guilty of the new poverty crimes that the government made a law recently," she pleaded to me with a parched voice as if I were the judge over her case.

"No one wanted to hear my excuses," the case worker told me at the DCPFS office. I was away from my children too much, and that was against the law. The case worker offered me a chance to visit my children in some kids' facility fifty miles outside of Freedom City in place called Dependence City, Sorrow said with her broken heart screaming louder than her words.

"I couldn't see them at home when I was working three jobs. There was no way I could have seen them fifty miles away every day. I love my kids, and I needed to be with them every minute of every second of the day. Their presence gave me the strength I needed to work three jobs and provide for them, but the lady wouldn't listen, and she had me escorted to the exit doors of the building with a court date to reappear before some judge the following year." She tapped on the table.

"I don't have any questions Ms. Sorrow, except did you go to the next court hearing?" I asked watching her mind leave reality and return to her chairs.

"Hey ya'll, I brought you some food for lunch. Are you hungry?" Ms. Sorrow asked the chairs.

Turning toward me, she looked at me strangely with her head tilted to the left and then to the right like she was making a judgment of me in some manner based on my silent attention to her every word. I don't think Ms. Sorrow has made up her mind about me, bad or good. Maybe she realized the history of her poverty has been given to a stranger and she has doubts about continuing to reveal it. When I got lost in my thoughts of pondering what her thoughts were with each continuing tilt of her head, she spoke.

"I left that building with so much pain in my heart, soul, head, and lungs forgot to expire and my legs became weak, and I stumbled down the stairs. I walked north in the direction of home, and I began to feel my feet tingle, then my knees tingled. The tingling feeling continued throughout my body, and after each tingle I no longer felt that body part. I didn't feel my feet or my legs, and I knew they were there because they had to carry me home. I didn't feel my heart, my head, or my lungs anymore—I didn't feel anything anymore."

"Walking home, left foot in front of the right, right foot in front of the left, I walked fifty miles into the numbness of this world away from America and No Where with water sneaking out of my eyes without my permission. With each tear, my Love joined me on the walk reminding me that tears are for joy only. I replied, 'There was no joy when we're absent from our kids.'" She was looking in my direction as if I were her husband.

She continued, "I was internally and physically numb to America's morality giving my mind permission to permanently leave my reality when I reached the door of our home. Instead of turning the knob, I turned and walked west and kept walking. There was no need for me to go home without my children and my husband, so there was no need for employment. They took my babies and made it impossible for me to ever be near them again," she said with anger boiling over in her soul, making her eyes red as she tapped the table.

"Ms. Sorrow, you may continue. I have no questions," I said with water filling my eyes as she reminded me of that powerless feeling against poverty that I have trying to provide for my children independent from welfare programs and this prison.

"Henrietta, take Hope and Happy to the bathroom and make sure their hands are clean from lunch please," she instructed before speaking to me again. "I walked left after right, right after left, with my feet hitting the pavement like a soundless drum until I decided to sleep wherever my body dropped. When my head hit the ground, I saw my Love telling me how proud he was to be my husband, restating his vows to me repeatedly until all four of my babies woke me up the following morning wanting breakfast. My family and I have been together every day for over a year, until one day, our walk was interrupted by an Officer Patience of the courts. He told us we were under arrest for living below poverty line and needing shelter from the state. We followed Officer Patience, and he took us to jail in America.

"He said the new poverty system was a long process, but eventually they would gather millions of homeless from both America and Freedom City and lock them away in No Where prisons all over the country. Since Officer Patience was the arresting officer at the scene of my poverty, he had to appear in court on the date of my trial. The court assigned us a public defender named Grace, who told us not to take the plea some woman named Supercilious would offer. Supercilious told us that we needed to choose from depression, substance abuse, prostitution, insanity, or suicide as a plea, or she would embarrass and humiliate my husband and children on the witness stand for living in poverty. All my family has is our honor, and Love always told me to never dishonor the family, so we took the insanity plea and returned to No Where, Freedom City." She tapped the table.

"Are you still numb?" I asked.

"Shhhhh, Happy and Hope, you're too loud coming back to this table, and we are in the library. I'll take you to the park in a minute to be as loud as you like, I promise," Sorrow said to her four children.

"Positive, is it?" Sorrow asked as if her mind had forgotten me.

"Yes, ma'am, it is, my name is Positive."

"Your mind can't grasp the pain I felt when my children were stolen from me. I couldn't grasp the pain, so I went numb to be with my family again. That is all those pleas are that Supercilious or any prosecutor offers. They're numbness, a way to not feel the painful realities of poverty or notice the disapproving looks from the judgment of people. Yes, I'm still numb, physically existing in No Where, but absent of my conscious determination to fight against the poverty system because I quit," answered Sorrow. She tapped the table.

8

I heard my children laughing so loud downstairs in the library with Escape that I knew I had been away from them for too long. Lucky enough to have spent an hour with Ms. Sorrow uninterrupted, I could not ask her anymore questions because my children were clearly unsupervised. "Excuse me, Ms. Sorrow and children, but I have to leave now. My loves are yearning for my attention. It was a pleasure meeting you, Ms. Sorrow, Love, Henry, Henrietta, Hope, and Happy," I said with a raspy voice from sharing tears of her story of poverty as I returned my chair to the other table.

"Henry gather your siblings together, we best be leaving also if we're going to enjoy the park before curfew," instructed Sorrow. "We'll see each other again, I'm sure," she said grabbing her bowl to balance on her head and exiting the library.

"Escape, why did you leave my kids downstairs alone?" I asked beginning to walk in her direction.

"How was your conversation with Crazy Lady, did you have fun?" Escape asked ignoring my question.

"She's not crazy, and our conversation wasn't fun, it was devastating. Why are you upstairs looking for a book with my children downstairs making all that noise in a library?" I repeated my question like she was deaf as I pushed passed her, running downstairs to them. The staircase wound down like a coiled spring, and the stairs decreased in width until the bottom step could fit only one of my feet, but two feet of a child-sized person.

"Those are not just your children making all that noise in a library. They're having fun for once," Escape argued in a whisper chasing me downstairs. "Whatever you do, go easy on them, you could use the music of their laughter in your soul right now, and they could use a memory of you smiling in their minds."

"I need you to stay in your zone of my life as a stranger who has a lot to learn from me and wants so desperately to be friends, not as a coparent," I said slowing down my pace as the sound of my children grew louder.

The books on the shelves were stiff and dusty, and the tables were small. This place looked like a dirty basement of books more than the lower level of a library. An Asian-looking man at the desk did not look up from his computer. He simply pointed me into the direction of the noise. The noise of children playing was deafening as I approached the room to discover a roar of laughter and see a burst of energy from my children as they chased each other up and down the unleveled carpeted floor, which was sectioned off in bright orange, yellow, red, green, and purple. I stood at the entrance of their fun watching as Content chased Reason, Strength tickled Peace, Truth jumped between the different colors of carpet on the floor while Harmony and Praise listened to an audio book. My creased forehead and frown of anger and annoyance with Escape's inability to monitor my children for a brief period subsided into a smooth smile. Staring at the excitement and free-spirit of my children, I too forgot we were in the library until the man from the desk encouraged me to do something about the noise or we would have to leave.

"Ug-hum," I cleared my throat. "What are you doing, is this the way we behave when I am not around?" I sternly questioned ready to play myself.

The room froze with seriousness and silence with all of shocked little eyes looking back at me in horror. Escape quickly moved around me rushing toward her kids who were standing in the yellow section of the room. Content watched Ms. Escape protect her children from my lecture and remained silent with her thoughts of explanation lost in the maze of her brain.

"Uh-oh, busted," exclaimed Reason and Truth.

"Please don't yell at them, it is my fault. When I came down here, I saw my two standing on the side of the table with confusion because your five were dusting books off they had not read and rereading books you used to teach them when ya'll lived in America. I thought that was a bit strict, and if your kids have been doing this all their little lives, then fun was overdue. You were upstairs doing what you wanted to do, so I was letting them do what they wanted to do for a change before you began your gruesome lessons with them. I asked the man at the desk if we could use this room, and their fun must have slipped into the ears of the whole library. I'm terribly sorry about the noise, but it's not their fault," Escape said in one breath. "It's mine," holding her arms in front of Praise and Harmony as if to protect them from my discipline.

"Tenemos que volver antes del toque de queda, obtener sus abrigos que es hora de irse. Ahora!"

"Lo siento, Mama, estamos llegando ahora," Content replied.

Escape motioned to her children to put their coats on and follow us upstairs. The youth area transformed from being a place of laughter back into the library with everyone's immediate silence and attention on me, awaiting the next instruction as we climbed the stairs to the main level of the library. Escape shook her head in disappointment that my children were silenced and leaving the library early.

"I know you're upset that they were loud, but are you really an enemy of fun?" Escape asked me as we walked out of the library. "They're going to be kids one time, and no matter what is going on in your adult life, you have one chance and one time to make their childhood an awesome experience," protested Escape turning left following us onto Independence Street.

"Escape, you decided to become a failure at life when you refused to try, try to become something you could be proud of, so spare me your lecture of Escape's parenting skills. I may not parent my children in a liberal way like you would prefer that I do, but I definitely don't encourage them to exist in life with no ambitions, failing to believe in themselves, but have fun. I am not a teacher of laziness, I refuse to encourage them to numb themselves with fun every time life's challenges present themselves. People numb themselves with your so-called fun every day when they give up in life. They numb themselves with the fun of drugs so they can no longer feel the pain of a broken heart. They numb themselves with the fun of alcohol to forget their hurtful memories, or with the fun of sex to pretend they are loved and appreciated for a short time within their long days of loneliness. I'm not raising my children to become acquainted with the fun of giving up, nor am I raising them to pacify their struggles with fun. I'm raising them to work through their struggles with a clear mind, to embrace hurt when it visits and press through it with hope that their lives will be better than the pain of yesterday, I lectured Escape turning right onto Way Out Street.

"Are you mad at the kids?" asked Escape. "Are you mad at me? Why must we walk all the way home in silence when it's such a beautiful day, even the ants aren't quiet as they work for their winter's rest. What is so bad about having a good time? Do you remember when you were a kid and how much fun that was, or in your case probably wasn't?" she asked with a pause realizing she had confused herself with the last question. "Are you always quiet when you're upset? Why do you shut people out of your little world when someone has fun? Does fun make you uncomfortable?" Escape continued to ask question after question of me until she saw the kids running toward the park.

Listening to the sigh of relief that came over Escape after she realized we took the kids to the park, I answered her previous questions. "It is not fun to be locked away in this reality of poverty's prison only existing as a middle class person in my imagination which motivates me to thrive off of the American persuasion that a higher education guarantees achieved prosperity. It is not fun to see your children locked out of well-deserved indulgences like braces on their teeth, or having their own house with their own rooms, yet encouraging your children that somehow we're going to leave poverty because I have a college degree like America required of me to obtain. It's not fun to see my kids achieve honor roll in private school that I could no longer afford, while promising them that their prayers will be answered because of their obedience and academic achievements year after year and heaven remains quiet.

"It's not fun to think you've met a decent man to marry when you really met an enemy of love, a heartbreaker. It's not fun to begin your adulthood as a single parent because an older man lies to you as a teenager. It's not fun to have an ex-husband who was too self-fish to participate in our family and waited for me to fail at college so he would have someone to blame for his fear to live. It's not fun when your ex-fiancé decides that our son and my inability to acquire employment in America in spite of my daily efforts and interviews were a plot to use him and his measly paychecks that he wouldn't have had without me. It's not fun listening to your ex-fiancé confess that he's been cheating on you while you're pregnant, then never come to the delivery of his son."

"It's not fun to have one last hope in a potential union that could have really worked for the sake of balancing the kids with two good parents ruined by the negative views of his family, so it was better that he ripped my heart out in a separation rather than remain with us doing the worst of times. It's not fun for my sons to repeatedly see bad examples of men with no integrity, morale, or loyalty to stand by their commitments. It's not fun to see the saints you grew up with and attended church with shun you like a stranger because they've sat and kept a record of your sins as a reminder to you when you come to fellowship."

"It's not fun to see your wonderful children wear the same clothes year after year and know if it had not been for God, my mother, and brother, their clothes would have fallen off them two years ago. It is not fun to later see your children wear yellow jumpers that label them as a plague of misfortune in all of their upcoming first impressions in Freedom City before their social lives begin to flourish. Not everyone enjoys poverty like you seem to, not everyone believes this place is their home," I said.

"Look around at the yellow jumpers in No Where, not everyone is proud to be born here, raised here, and return here because they are afraid that if they try to be anything in life, their brain will explode from just the idea. So no, Escape, I don't have a problem with fun, I

77

just know what fun isn't," I howled with tears. "And yes, I don't want my loves to ever laugh in this place or run around with anyone's kids in this place resembling any type of enjoyment or contentment, because we are not staying in No Where being nothing."

Calling the kids over to us from the playground, Escape began isolating her children from mine. "What's wrong, Mom?" Praise asked Escape.

"Nothing," she said looking at me with tears in her eyes. She backed away from me in silence until her family was no longer in my sight.

"Mom, we aren't friends with Ms. Escape anymore. are we?" asked Peace, "Why was Ms. Escape crying?"

"I guess tears aren't for joy after all," I replied, picking up the twins as we left the park.

9

"Momma, you have to take your shot now," mumbled Strength as to not disturb my thoughts and prevent any remembrance of the Old Library to surface in my mind for fear of punishment. I accepted the bag with my shot and gave them all instructions to bathe before I prepared dinner so they could go straight to bed after they ate. Putting the shot into the chamber, I rolled up my sleeve and injected it into the fleshy part of my forearm. Then I dosed off for just a minute. Then I woke up to Reason and Truth snuggled under me and a smell from the kitchen that woke up a growl in my stomach.

"How long was I sleeping this time?"

"You only slept for an hour," said Content. "Are we really in trouble for the Old Library?" she asked as she prepared the dinner plates anxiously waiting for my answer.

Glancing down at Truth and Reason, I yawned, "No." While I was speaking, I heard screams and glass shatter in the distance. My children froze in fear, and I sneaked a peek out the window directly into a serious confrontation of a gray jumper being forced to relocate to the Valley. My heart sank into my feet, and fear moved to where my heart used to be. The gray jumper must have been indicted without a plea. An officer Future motioned me to stay away from the window, and I had to come up with an explanation to calm my children's fears. "That was just a misunderstanding, it seems someone was given the wrong jumper," I said. "What did you cook?" I asked Content looking at all of my children begin to relax after noticing my slight smile.

"We are having chicken and peas, you are having peas mom," Content replied with a moan as she scooped the peas in disgust, placing them on each plate.

"Is the food ready?" Peace asked.

"Yep, and it's delicious" replied Strength as she grabbed a piece of chicken out of the pot.

With the sounds of chewing that filled the kitchen, I would agree with Strength the dinner was delicious. I have great kids, I thought, watching them help the twins keep the peas on their spoon. "Think Mom and Miss Escape are going to remain friends?" asked Peace.

"I don't know. It's hard to tell if they're going to be friends after all the hollering at the park today," said Content.

"I think they're going to be the best of friends, at least Mom had better be friends with Ms. Escape, or she's going to have answer to me," Strength said as she stood on a chair pretending to be an adult.

"I'll remember to report directly to you," I said startling Strength to almost falling off the chair. "You all go to bed, I will finish the cleaning. We do have an early wakeup call," I reminded them after receiving a strong hug from Strength before they went upstairs. I walked to the kitchen sink and nearly jumped into the ceiling when I turned around to see Content standing behind me. "Girl, I'm going to get some bells for those ankles of yours, how may I help you?" I asked with my heart rate trying to return to its normal speed.

"Sorry Mom, you left your shot dispenser on the floor, and I didn't want the twins to get it, so I was giving it to you," she answered holding the dispenser in her hand smiling with pride that her walk and presence are fearfully quiet.

"Never mind my shot dispenser, go to bed" I said.

"Does that mean we can play with Harmony and Praise tomorrow?" asked Content while I heard Peace and Strength on the steps waiting on my response.

"Nice try. My dispenser has no meaning, it's an object. And if Ms. Escape will permit them to play with you tomorrow after what I said to her earlier today, maybe we'll go to the park. How's that?" I asked.

"Yes! Yesss, yes!" Peace and Strength cheerfu.
the stairs.

"Glad I could make ya'll happy again. Now go
and I'll see ya'll at wakeup call," I insisted.

Turning off the lights in the kitchen and sitting or.
the living room, I thought about what Ms. Sorrow saia
family and her fight against poverty. I remembered the words of n.
Escape, the distress call of fun from my children, and how she used to
believe she found a friend in me until I had to show her the reality of
her imagination of this prison; Now, that Escape can see to my reality
of this fun-less prison, I'm sure we're strangers again.

Killing the roaches and other bugs on the floor with a shoe, I
just laid here, looking up at the ceiling, wondering if God began listening to my thoughts or preferred that I didn't speak to him. Maybe
I should stop killing these critter companions of the cell so I'd have
something to talk to, or hope an angel overhears my thoughts and
prayers reporting them to God for me. I have been in poverty for
years, we've been in exile of descent living before this prison, and I
want out. "Help," I yelled quietly as to not wake up my kids. "Get
us out of here, I just want out of here, let me out before I become so
obsessed with leaving this place it causes me to go insane."

My children amaze me at how quickly they choose to forgive
and forget. It hasn't been two days since my argument with Escape
and they want to make friends with her kids and play in the library
more than they want to learn from me at the moment. My mind
can't stop replaying my life sentence verdict despite my education I
achieved during the gruesome years of trial. And if that's not enough,
thoughts of my ex-fiancé visit me, it's all craziness and I don't want to
play with either of them, court or my ex-fiancé.

* * *

"Rise and shine, rise and shine," sang Officer Future outside my window. "You know the drill, you have two hour before we see you outside," added Officer Future as he left our window singing "Rise and
Shine."

Loves, are you awake and has everyone eaten something?" elled upstairs after listening to their feet moving around on the oors.

"Yes, we are all awake and dressed, and no, we did not eat anything, so I hope you cooked breakfast," reported Strength.

"You are too young to have such a big mouth with me, Strength. There are some apples and toast in a plate on the counter. Eat quickly so we can get outside, I don't want to deal with any officers today or the famous Lady Lost," I said running upstairs to the shower.

"Mom, you have five minutes left before outside call, hurry up" yelled Content.

"I'm coming, I'm coming," I responded at the same time the bolts unlocked.

Content opened the door to the sun's usual bright greeting and to Lady Lost on the intercom giving her detested instructions to the residents as we were coming outside to join the rest of the cellmates in idleness. She exclaimed, "I am tired of all the window repairs we have to make around here because the white jumpers decide they don't like windows in fights, drug parties, fits of unwarranted rage, and residential reassignments. Therefore, whoever breaks another window attempting to get sympathy from the medics and hospital because you're needy, I'm going to look into turning your water off, then your lights, then your gas. When I get done with you, you'll want to be cold and stiff," Lady Lost guaranteed before the intercom shut off.

"Mom, we're going to Ms. Escape's cell to see if she wants to go to the park with us today, okay?" Strength asked hoping to receive approval.

"You're not going anywhere in here by yourselves, and if Ms. Escape wants her children to play with you all, we're not lost, they know where to find us," I bellowed out to them as they tried to run to Ms. Escape's cell before they received my approval at the same time Grace approached our cell.

"Good morning, Positive, how did you rest last night?" he asked.

"I stopped resting five years ago. What are you doing here in land of the forgotten?" I asked, noticing he was wearing jeans and a jacket rather than the standard court suit.

"You refuse to take my calls, so I decided to visit you and the kids. I'm doing my best to help, but you make it impossible when you don't answer the phone. This is the only trip out here I can make, so I hope you will be more cooperative, please," Grace stated in attempt to derail an argument from me.

"It must be nice to only have to visit a prison and leave at your leisure," I said, watching all the residents stare at him. "My loves want to go play, so we made park plans. Sorry you wasted a drive here, I groaned."

"You are going to allow them to be children today," smirked Grace. "I believe it's good that you're allowing them to be children before their childhood is put away and they become adults. Where is your friend Ms. Escape?"

"She is not my friend. I was her friend by her statement and probably not anymore after I lectured her about having an ambition for the sake of her kids. How do you know Escape?" I asked.

Before Grace could respond to my question, Escape approached my cell. "It's a beautiful day out," Miss Escape spoke loudly, drawing everyone's attention to her usual the "The Sun Will Come Out Tomorrow" anthem every morning.

"I guess since everything is still beautiful to you. You'll be joining us for a walk to the park? I asked.

"Not interested in going with you anywhere unless you're inviting us," Escape said as she formerly introduced herself to Grace, who knew her prior to this visit. "Hi, my name is Escape, and you are?"

"We are inviting you," interrupted Truth and Reason in unison, keeping a low tone as to not upset me.

"Harmony, Praise, and I would love to join ya'll. Where are we going?" Escape asked the twins.

"They're going to the park, Mama," Praise interrupted. "Content and Strength just said so." With a look of irritation on my face, I asked Escape if she and her children wanted to join us at the park today.

"Yes, Positive, we would be delighted to join your educated family at the park today," she said annoyed by my interruption of her introduction to Grace.

"My name is Grace, I'm Positive's attorney," he said with a very professional tone.

"Cut the crap," I demanded. "He asked about you three minutes before you came over here, so you both know each other, stop faking with the first introduction please," I insisted.

"Actually, in prison it's not difficult to discover who the inmates have become acquaintances with. By word of mouth, I heard Ms. Escape and you were friends, so I researched her file in protection of you. No offense Ms. Escape. This is my first time meeting her in person," Grace said.

"No offense taken," Escape replied walking with us exiting from Effort Hill. We walked in silence mostly listening to the laughter of the kids until we reached the park when Grace decides to enlighten us on the recent history of the park's landscape.

"Did you know this is the biggest park in Freedom City because it's designed to separate the poverty lifers from the citizens?" he asked. "You both have to use the park, but the prison side is here on the East, and the citizen's side is on the West. The bathrooms, drinking fountains, Athenian statues, and water monuments are in the center of the park that separate the two, and citizens get preferential treatment if you both have to use any of the facilities at the same time," he added with a smile feeling proud of his tour.

"Positive, did you know there are Poverty Crow laws to this park?" asked Grace.

"Wow! Poverty Crow laws in a park, I didn't know there was a law against being poor and playing in a free park," I replied to Grace. "Poverty is not a contagious disease any different than the race of a person is contagious to a different culture of people, you can't die from it. What did you need to speak with me about that was so urgent you came here?" I asked Grace.

"Why don't we talk over here at the picnic table and let Escape babysit the children while they play?" suggested Grace.

"I'm not a baby, and neither are my brothers and sisters," replied Truth and Reason.

"Forgive me, the young adults can play, how's that?" asked Grace smiling.

"Don't mind us, we'll be over here so you two can finish your business," interrupted Escape.

The picnic table was old cracked wood, missing the bolts that stabilized it to the ground. Grace sat across from me taking out a notepad with scribbling on it.

"Positive, you should write a letter to the parole board, and I will help you complete your commutation form. It is important that we get this completed before the next year because Governor Forgiving will have five new members and a new elected chairman that are elected every five years. You were sentenced almost a year ago, and this parole board would be more likely to remember your case from all the letters you sent to court appealing for a retrial, which are public record. I'm sure one of the members, if not all of them, have read your numerous requests to court or have done some type of research on the inmates when their number is up," he said with eagerness.

"Don't remind me of my numerous letters I wrote to the court. The judge kept sending me a response that she had received it and that this matter was no longer handled in court. I received so many of those letters with identical wording that I began to think the judge did not read them at all or could not read and just stamped them with a received date to be carted off to the inmate archives or something. Now you're telling me in order for my requests to be considered, I have to get the attention of the parole board? What can the parole board do for me?" I questioned.

"Should the parole board agree or sympathize with your request of parole, then your letter will be passed to Governor Forgiving to rule on their recommendation for your parole. However, the governor won't acknowledge your letter or any documents that you submit if the parole board doesn't make a recommendation on your behalf," explained Grace.

"What do I have to do exactly?" I asked watching my children play. I noticed a couple approaching them at the drinking fountain.

The couple wasn't from No Where because they were not wearing jumpers. They wore expensive material from some expensive store. The clothes would have looked beautiful had it not been for the scowl on their faces as they were speaking to my children.

"Hold on, Grace, my loves need me," I said abruptly before he could respond. "Excuse me. Is there a problem over here?" I said quickly approaching the drinking fountains that were enclosed by brick around two centered pipes of water that flowed at the drinkers' command with the turn of a handle. Escape was yelling something that was unclear at the top of her lungs the closer I drew to them. Peace saw me and immediately began explaining the problem in Spanish.

"Estas personas no quieran Señorita Armonía para compartir la fuente de agua potable con sus hijos, el malicia y la envidia," Peace muttered. Peace spoke with a low voice in the midst of any trouble he could sense, and he was glad he spoke a different language because he avoided arguments with children who had no understanding of Spanish to respond.

"Look, everyone can drink from these fountains, and if you feel like your children shouldn't share with our children, then they may wait their turn," I said directly to the parents.

"I don't know who or what you used to be in America, seeming how your son speaks another language, but for whatever the reason, America has outlawed you as criminal inmates, so act like inmates and refrain your children from drinking until our children have quenched their thirst," the woman argued.

"I would understand your point if you wouldn't have outlawed yourselves from America as penniless retirees, that's why you're sharing Freedom City with us," I interrupted walking closer to the woman, but the lady continued as I walked around the fountain and stood closer to the woman keeping her in my arms' reach.

"Read the sign on the monuments, the bathroom, and this fountain beneath. If the citizens and prisoners ever want to use the facilities at the same time, the citizens are privy to going first," pointed out the mother, whose name is Greed, Escape whispered to me out of breath from running across the park.

"Who are you that the fountains are that important to you? I'm guessing nobody because there are far greater things to fight over than a water fountain. Ya'll nobodies with nothing else to do with your time in Freedom City same as us," I said looking directly at Greed while Grace was trying to nudge me away from them.

"My name is Bitter, and this is my wife Greed," interjected Bitter. "Now are you going to tell your kids to move, so ours can drink from this fountain, or do we have to report you to No Where?" he asked observing Escape's attempt to pull me away from them.

I could feel heat rising from a MS flare up burning me on a cellular level. This confrontation was just what I needed to blow off some steam. "Positive, officers Future are coming across the park," Escape said lowly. "The park has cameras, this whole city has cameras," Escape added. When Grace saw the officers drawing closer to the fountains, he began to diffuse the situation diplomatically, stepping in front of me.

"Dejar la fuente de agua potable solo y salir a jugar, se puede beber agua en el hogar," I instructed to my children.

My children began to walk away from the fountain, and Escape's family just followed mine because they didn't understand a word of Spanish.

"Supongo que eso es lo que hacemos ahora, nos alejamos y dejar que los ricos tienen todo," mumbled Content and Strength with sad countenances.

"Mrs. Greed and Mr. Bitter, you are right, the kids have left the fountain so your malice and envy may wet their throats. There should be no hard feelings, and no one needs to report anyone at this point, correct?" Grace asked with an urgency.

"As long as they know their place and you keep them in their place, there is no need for a report," agreed Bitter seconds before the officers arrived at the fountain.

"Is there a problem here today?" Officer Future asked the citizens.

"No, there isn't a problem over here. Our kids were getting a drink of water before these inmates. They're almost done, and the fountain will be free to them in a moment," responded Bitter, encouraging the officers to leave the park.

It was one thing to know that we did not belong in No Where, but it was mind-alarming to see that Freedom City had uncompassionate, hateful people, and the accumulation of wealth and prestige were not the cause, but poverty survival before they too became No Where inmates was the cause of their inhumane behavior.

"Since when did education and money give anyone the right to treat No Where residents as unimportant and inexistent when the only thing that separates us from the citizens is information in a book, or in my case money?" I asked Grace.

"I don't know when it happened," answered Grace smiling at me as if he had seen something pleasant within my anger. "Positive, I have to leave immediately when we return. I will call you again, and I expect you to answer," he said trying to keep up with our walking pace that I've built up to over the months.

"Whatever, Grace, I don't trust you anymore. Maybe I will answer or maybe I will not, I'm not making you any promises. Right now, I need to get back and deal with my loves' events from today because they shouldn't have to walk away from anything or anyone because they live in poverty. Poverty has been an unrelenting curse over the past seven years in their lives and I'm focused on keeping poverty mentality out of their minds," I said to Grace as he climbed inside his truck.

"Answer the calls Positive," Grace persisted. "I will have to give you the information that is needed for your commutation over the phone," he said backing his truck into the street.

"Have better days than mine," I said to Grace as he drove out of Effort Hill, ignoring his phone call request of me.

"Are you going to answer his calls now?" Escape asked, "He seems like he's going to get you out of here to me," she added.

"All men appear to be committed to a common suffering to some degree until they decide to betray you and save themselves," I replied. "I don't have any confidence in Grace. Look at where we ended up when I believed him the first time. Why should the second time be any different?" I asked.

"Think about changing your mind about Grace, really think about it," Escape said on her way into Registration for her food vouchers before the food delivery arrived.

10

"Positive, you have a phone call. Positive, you have a phone call. Report to Registration immediately," Lady Lost requested through the intercom. Watching Positive and her children walk directly past Registration toward the food delivery line of people ignoring Lady Lost's request, I became interested in who called Positive so frequently. I think it's time for me to visit Registration. Who knows? Something good might come of living in No Where temporarily before the prosecutor can indict me with robbery, theft, and poverty. My children and I could be citizens of America again. Answering that call today, would at least give me something do in this boring place before I go mad from being in the company of broke people, I thought, talking myself into answering her call without getting caught.

Opening the door of Registration, I saw Lady Lost in the office across from the phone that hung upside down off the hook. I saw the working residents who were busy sorting vouchers and other tasks, they didn't notice I had entered or that I picked up the phone.

"Hello," I answered.

"Hello, Positive, is that you?"

"Yes."

"Where have you been? I have been calling for weeks since my visit out there," Grace said.

"No Where."

"Very amusing," Grace said sarcastically. "I'm glad you're in a better mood than the last time we spoke," he continued, rambling on and on about waiting patiently and believing that there is always a way out.

"What way out? You found a sure way out of here?" I asked trying to remember to keep my answers short and quiet.

"Yes, you know I found a way out. We talked about this at the park, remember?" he asked. "The time is running out on the phone now, thanks to your stroll to answer it, so we will have to talk another time. Make sure you're timely answering the phone next time, and I'll go through the details with you next time."

"No problem," I replied. "Before you go, what time should I expect your next call?" I asked, searching for a pen and paper on a nearby resident's desk stretching the phone cord.

"That's odd, you never wanted to know when I would be calling you before," he commented. "I will call you next week, you and the kids keep laughing." Grace said soothingly just before the call ended.

He found a way out of here, and it will be just what I need, I'm sure of it, I thought. *This is the easiest plan I ever made. I just answered someone else's call. How brilliant is that?* I asked myself feeling another hand on top of mine when we hung the phone up together. Turning around to see who hung the phone up with me, hoping it wasn't Positive. I stared directly into the eyes of Lady Lost.

"Come into my office now, a meeting is scheduled for you to meet with me now," Lady Lost said viperously soft, causing all the residents to turn their attention to her because she rarely spoke without howling.

Following Lady Lost into her office, I chose to remain standing rather than sitting in the chair she offered. Silence is bad for my nerves, I wish this chick would hurry up and present her proposal for the phone call info.

"Ms. Deceitful Ways, correct?" she asked, with her eyes questioning whether or not I would comply with whatever she was up to.

"Yes, that's my name," I answered.

"Where are your children while you are in Registration answering the call for another resident?" she inquired.

"They are outside our cell where you put them when you announced outside call this fine early morning," I replied watching her play with her pen on the desk.

"Fine," she said, "I was trying to respect what is left of you before you become my Valley resident soon after Ms. Supercilious finds you guilty of poverty," she proclaimed, annoyed with her failed attempt at sneaky small talk.

"How do you know who my prosecutor is?" I asked.

"Poor child, this is why you should have went to school. You came here on the bus the same night as Positive. There is only one prosecutor assigned to the states of Kansas, Missouri, Illinois, and Kentucky. Besides the fact that I have your papers, you had to have come from one of those states."

"What is it that I can do for you?" I asked while looking down at her small world of authority because she has a little desk, chair, file cabinet, and phone. Everything was small to fit her very small mind.

"You can do something for me and I can do something for you, and that is what this little emergency meeting is about," she continued. "I want you to continue to answer Grace's calls for Positive," requested Lady Lost. "I don't have to suggest keeping Grace's information to yourself because you were going to do that anyway."

"And what is the something you are going to do for me?" I asked looking as Lady Lost sat up in her chair getting excited on the notion that she would have a successful meeting.

"I will make a call to the prosecutor's office and persuade them to look into another citizen in a different state because you are at least present in the prison not causing debt at the moment. I will remind Supercilious of her workload and urgency to annihilate debt caused by the lazy poor citizens who procreate and are unable to substantiate self-sufficiency," she said with confidence as she intercrossed her fingers.

"What is in this for you?" I asked.

"Deceitful, honey, please remember that I make a living—"

"On the cold and stiff," we said in unison. Then she picked up her glass of water for a sip like she was giving me a speech.

"For someone who detest repetition, your conversation seems full of it. I know you make a living off of us. How exactly do you make your living off of us?" I asked.

"Please sit, stay a while. Would you like anything to drink before I answer your complicated question?"

Sitting in the chair in front of her desk, I prepared myself to listen with my legs crossed at the knees and hands placed gently on my lap. Watching her envy my long legs and tantalizing movements that define womanhood, I waited patiently for her answer.

"Look, pretty girl, let this be the only time you ever question me," Lady Lost stated between the grit of her teeth. When a Valley member is cold and stiff, I get them in the earth immediately, letting them bother whatever is on the other side of death with their excuses of living inefficiently. The prosecutor's office is government funded to enforce this new law, and they pay me for my loyalty to rid America of the weakest citizens. Their mission is to get America out of debt by cutting their costs and losses of the poor.

"How much do you earn off the cold and stiff exactly?" I interrupted hoping to get as much information on her operation as possible since she feels vulnerable and needs my help.

"None of your business," Lady Lost replied, "but it's enough to keep me out of poverty for a lifetime, she bragged as she continued. "Think back, you should be old enough to remember when the government began a demolition project of all low-income housing in the local poor neighborhoods. They began giving the poor vouchers to live in homes they had built across the nation, but the catch was the adults had to maintain employment to pay their utilities bills, rent, or mortgage. When, the poor gained income they used it to maintain their new homes in order to fulfill the stipulations required to remain a member of the voucher program. Their ability to remain in the voucher program caused a decline in their medical benefits and food stamp allowance from the welfare program to nearly no assistance, based on their income levels.

"Consequently, the poor would have homes temporarily and no medical or food benefits that they could afford, so they began living without it. Well, you can see what the result was of that because you're standing in my office before me now in their new program."

"Are you saying their new program is for anyone who lives in poverty or below the line of poverty will receive a sentence to life in No Where, which is actually death because you're waiting on them to become cold and stiff?" I asked.

"You're a smart lady after all, and I prefer the words 'cold and stiff,' it sounds better that way, so don't use the d-word in my presence again. Yes, that is the shorter version of explaining the new program. It's easier for our government to be responsible for my income and needs than it is to be responsible for over 45 million poor, give or take a few thousand incomes and needs."

Sitting there in awe, stunned that the government is disposing poor people down a drain of inexistence like trash, like a garbage disposal, and realizing me and my children are one of those next in line to be disposed of made me ill. "I think I'm going to be sick." I hurled in the trash can she put in front of my face.

"Get control of yourself. I don't clean, and vomit is disgusting. You have nothing to worry about as long as you answer the calls and report to me," Lady Lost said handing me a Kleenex.

"What does all of this have to do with Positive?"

"Poor girl, I was just beginning to think you were one of the smart ones, even if you didn't go to school, insulted Lady Lost. My income is derived from the cold and stiff, so it is my goal to never allow any of you to return to America. If some of you manage to leave from No Where and become accepted as citizens in America, I lose thousands out of my paycheck. And if I lose thousands, the rest of you will lose vouchers until my rage returns to this pleasant person you see sitting before you now." She smiled grimly.

"I understand, no problem, I can continue to answer Positive's calls for as long as you like, but my children and I will get additional food and water every month," I negotiated.

"I can do that. I will increase your voucher amounts," she agreed.

"Then you have a deal. Should we shake on it?" I asked not telling her of my plans to use her and anyone else to return to America, the place where I get any and every one to do for me, my paradise.

Lady Lost grabbed my hand in a grip like she was squeezing lemons. "A person's word is all anyone has in this world, remember that. I'm taking your word that you will do your part," she said as she walked me to her door, telling one of her residents to give me two vouchers additional for the month.

I exited her office with my mind wheeling over the possibilities that my stay here could be the shortest Lady Lost has ever witnessed since the government employed her. I took my vouchers and walked out of Registration to Lady Lost's voice beckoning a few officers Past for a meeting.

11

In a hurry for my vouchers before the Foody Truck came, I ran down the hill, crossed the street and onto the sidewalk bumping into several Valley members by accident. Finally reaching Registration, panting out of breath, I opened the door to Ms. Deceitful smiling as she exited. No one smiles about having food vouchers or having to be anywhere near Ms. Lady Lost, so what was she smiling for? I wondered. *No time for that*, I thought, *I have to get those vouchers*.

"Hi, I'm here for my vouchers," I reported to a resident's desk.

He looked up at me and returned his eyes to his list of names. "I have your vouchers Escape, next time be here early. When you're late you miss the walls talking," the resident said.

"I miss the walls talking? What are you talking about?" I asked. "You are wearing the yellow jumper, so I won't think you're crazy yet. Please, may I have my vouchers? The truck will be here in less than twenty minutes," I begged the resident.

"My name is Deliverance, and that is what you call me, soldier. I may be wearing a yellow jumper but it's not my identity, and I'm far from crazy," he said stiffly as if he were ready to salute me. "Furthermore," he continued," I'm just trying to help you and your new friend out. Pay attention and remember what I said, the walls talk, and you missed the conversation." Deliverance insisted that I remember his words before handing $300 worth of vouchers to me.

"Okay, whatever, the walls talk and I missed the conversation, and somehow you are helping me and my new friend out. I promise to think about what you said later after I get the food," I said leaving

Registration in a hurry and running through the Valley as I heard the Foody Truck's engine turn on and saw it beginning to pull off toward Effort Hill. I took a short cut through an alley of cells rather than the street, and I arrived in time to stand in line behind Deceitful with Positive joining the line three residents behind me. I'm normally not a nosey person, but I couldn't help but notice Deceitful had $600 worth of food vouchers she handed when I saw the driver. That's a lot of food when we're given $300 a voucher the first week, and $200 a voucher every week after that until the month ends. Why has her voucher been doubled to begin the month with? I wondered. "You and your kids are going to eat good this week," I commented loud enough for others to notice my observance, but not loud enough that Deceitful would feel her flawless image of innocence was being challenged.

"Lethargic, carry these bags because they're the heaviest, Jealousy and Fear carry the drinks," instructed Deceitful. "I'm sorry, were you saying something to me?" She asked acting like I'm only visible when she acknowledges me.

"No, I was thinking out loud, never mind what I said. My name is Escape, and you are?" I introduced myself pretending to be ignorant of who she was and why she was in No Where.

"I know your name. Everyone knows your name, Escape. Stop with the fake politeness, you don't like me, and I don't care for you. Focus on you and your children, don't concern yourself with my vouchers, and we won't have any problems. Understood?" asked Deceitful squaring her shoulders off with mine as if to invoke fear in me. "Before I go," she added, "never mind that last statement," as she took her items and left the line walking across the street in the direction of her cell.

"Whatever," I replied loudly. Everyone here seems to think they are smarter than me. I'm tired of being mistreated because I like to befriend other residents. Deceitful and Positive act like they could exist alone here in the solitude of their minds until a plan of escape presents itself. Fine, they don't need a friend or conversation with me, and I don't need it from them either. I picked out the food I wanted as Praise and Harmony approached to help me exit the line. Positive and her children were almost next in line to gather their food, when I walked past them silently. My mind is made up, if Positive doesn't want to be my friend, that's cool, but she should have told me to leave her alone and that she doesn't want to be friends with me. She didn't have to be annoyed by our company. I asked her every time about sharing the day together. If she didn't want to, that is all she should have said, I thought while I waited to enter my cell. Sometimes, I don't like initiating every conversation with my so-called friends or visiting them all the time. When does anyone visit us or greet us in the mornings? I spoke out loud.

"Momma, what are you talking about?" asked Praise.

"Can we go play with Ms. Positive's kids?" requested Harmony.

"We don't play with Ms. Positive's kids anymore," I answered Harmony satisfied with my decision to refrain from being friends with residents who refuse my friendship.

"Momma, why don't we play with Ms. Positive kids anymore?" asked Harmony.

"People have to want to be friends, they have to make an effort to be friends even when they're not feeling friendly, and Positive doesn't want a friend. She wants someone she can vent her misery to, she wants to complain about her educational accomplishments not working and employment failures only," I answered my daughter at the sounds of the bolt unlocking and officers Present yelling, their night call.

Watching my children eat and laugh soothed the pain of my heart from the uncertainty of Positive's friendship. Harmony and Praise took their showers and went to bed for the night. Listening to their good nights to each other, I went downstairs to clean our mess from dinner. I cleaned the living room first and began to clean the kitchen when I remembered what Deliverance said: "You missed the walls talking." I missed the walls talking? What was Mr. Deliverance trying to tell me? It's hard to know if he was seriously talking to me or having a PTSD moment.

* * *

I was in the Iraq War serving America as a young man. There are some things in this world no one should ever see. War is a spiritual battle no mind could fight. Seeing a person's spirit in their bodies talking and laughing with you, and then watching their bodies fall limp when the spirit exits immediately within seconds after bullet contact, could make any mind insane. It was like spirits were visible in soldiers, and they departed with every bomb or bullet fired. Death greeted their bodies without a welcoming invitation, their souls released immediately. Yes, I suffer from PTSD, posttraumatic stress disorder, where my mind has a tendency to play ping-pong between the realities of my present and the memories of war, with a mixture of past hurt and present solitude.

When I returned from the war back in 2011, it took me a while to adjust to the calmness of my home and family. It's sad to say that, by the time I made the adjustment and gained 70 percent of the control over my war flashbacks, my wife divorced me and took everything. My veteran's benefits and monthly allowances were deposited to my bank timely, but it wasn't enough for me to survive wheeling around in America's constant inflation of taxes and paying child support to my ex-wife. I voluntarily signed up to live in No Where.

Living here is not nearly as bad as living in a foreign country where kids are trained to commit suicide and could kill you as a planned casualty when you are attempting to move them out of harm's way. No Where is a prison when you consider the routine officers everywhere and the poor conditions of this place in relation to the heart of a person like Positive, who desires to live better without being corrupted by sugar daddies, prostitution, drug dealing, and all the other uncountable evils of the world. I work in Registration for Lady Lost and keep to myself which is just the way I like it.

The night Positive and her family arrived, I gave her children the jumpers because she seemed to be in a state of shock or depression, refusing to accept the reality process of her deportation from America to No Where. Observing her sedated behavior, I was certain she didn't volunteer to live here. A person who is sedated in order to adjust to the new conditions they find themselves in is a good indication that you are in the presence of a fellow solider, in this case a young lady with a lion's heart that won't be tamed by the power drunk government's representatives who can't see beyond the greediness of their own pockets.

* * *

Yeah, that is it, I agree with my first thought, Deliverance was having a PTSD moment, which is the only reason for his twisted riddle. Cleaning the bathroom after taking my shower. Why am I considering his words all night if he was having a PTSD moment? I wondered. Seriously, I should be questioning my own sanity for considering what Deliverance said, he who is two steps from being as crazy as Ms. Sorrow. I missed the talking walls. No, I missed the walls talking. That's what he said, I think. Only thing is walls don't talk; this man is as loony as Ms. Sorrow, and he's going to make me a loon-goon too with his idea of talking walls. I'm going to bed.

12

"Positive, you have a call in Registration. Positive, you have call in Registration," announced Lady Lost. My children and I walked passed Registration and onto the Old Library.

"Momma, why don't you answer the call in Registration?" asked Peace.

"Because she doesn't want to and she doesn't have to," answered Strength with a smile as she felt proud of herself when she believed her answer was correct.

"My not wanting to answer the call is not because I'm being stubborn," I said looking at Strength. "I'm not answering the call because I need to rebuild my energy for the fight against an enemy as great as poverty, and my energy comes from being around all five of you and watching you learn what I teach in the library. So pay attention to the lessons, and I will continue to get stronger," I bribed.

My children enjoyed coming to the Old Library. The twins raced upstairs to the door, but neither of them could win because they patiently waited for each other. Entering the library, my children proceeded downstairs ahead of me because they heard old Ms. Sorrow calling me again.

"Psst, psst!" she whispered to me, and looking out the window like she didn't know where the sound was coming from.

"Hi, Ms. Sorrow, how can I be of service to you today?" I asked careful not to choose a chair to sit in that might be a family member.

"Henry, sit there in silence, you have done enough bothering your sister this morning," she instructed before tapping the table.

"Um, Ms. Sorrow you called me over here, so what's so important?"

"Henry if you don't sit still, you won't get any of that cake I baked this morning," she threatened her child in the seat closest to the window before looking in my direction. "When is the last time you've been to Registration?" she asked and then tapped the table.

"I haven't been to Registration in a couple of months. I have no need right now to visit Registration. Content, my oldest daughter, retrieves our vouchers every week for me and my injection, why?" I asked.

"Henrietta, you see what your brother is doing? Get a napkin, clean all of the saliva off the window. You know better, Happy. You know you're not supposed to draw on the window," she said. "He's trying to irritate me today, and it won't work. The only person that will be irritated is him when we're home eating cake without him," Sorrow said with a smile as she looked at me. "Someone has to answer those calls that ring for you, and if you're not answering them, then who?" she tapped the table.

"Lady Lost answers the calls, Ms. Sorrow. She told me she's not my secretary, and she would reduce my allowance until I answer the calls. My vouchers are the same every month, some good, her threat did to us," I said with pride.

"Kids, ya'll get ready to go for a walk. I like to breathe in the fresh air of people who are smart," she said looking toward me with disappointment and pushing the chairs in from where her children sat, and then turning toward me. "Ask yourself this one question: if you haven't answered the phone calls after Lady Lost threatened you, and your food allowance has not decreased, then who is answering your calls, smartest one in No Where?" With that, Ms. Sorrow left the library with her family, frowning at me like I should be ashamed of myself.

I sat there thinking about what Ms. Sorrow said before I went downstairs to teach my children their lesson for the day. As I neared the steps, I decided to ask Content about our vouchers.

"Content, baby, come here," I said while the twins were running toward me in a race against her.

"Yes, ma'am," responded Content.

"Our vouchers last week, what was the amount of our vouchers last week?" I asked.

"They were $200 last week because it was the last week of the month, and they were $300 this week because it's the first week of the month. They are the same amount they've always been," replied Content.

That is what I was afraid of. Ms. Sorrow was right. If I was not answering the calls, then who? I told my loves they had a free day from learning today, and it was time to leave the Old Library immediately. My children looked at me confused about the sudden change of plans today, but they didn't question it because they wanted to play all day anyway.

* * *

"Positive, I want you to sit and write the parole board a compelling letter about your life. I want you to explain that the outcomes of your poor choices in your personal life never stopped your decision to become a productive citizen, that you kept striving to do better by obtaining a trade, and degrees in traditional education, that you provided for your children through any legal suggestion that was given to you," Grace said. "Make them see that it is poverty that hinders your upward mobility, not laziness," he continued as he went through his list of things he wanted Positive to do before November of this year in less than five months.

"I hear you, Grace, write a good letter," said Deceitful looking at her nails.

"I hope you are taking my instructions seriously because you need to do this before November," he reiterated. "The parole board will change their members and chairman every five years, so this year is your chance to be heard by people who may know of your case since you recently were incarcerated," added Grace.

"I heard you the first time, is there anything else?" asked Deceitful as she put her hands on her hip waiting to end the call.

"Yes, you have been there almost a year now with no trouble, keep it that way. The parole board will consider your conduct in

No Where as a determinant for how you will behave should you be allowed to live in America again," he said.

"No problem, write a letter and stay out of everyone's way, and I could be released soon, I got it," said Deceitful before hanging up the phone.

"Good girl," said Lady Lost. "I will need to keep Positive from discovering that her freedom rests in a letter and good behavior. Your voucher increase will be ready next week as agreed," she promised Deceitful with a corrupt smile.

Deceitful shook Lady Lost's hand. I witnessed some agreement between the two of them when I opened the door. *Why would Deceitful and Lady Lost shake hands?* I thought, breathing hard from the run here from the Old Library. My children remained standing outside waiting for me to finish my business in Registration so they could play.

Walking into Registration with sweat pouring from my head trying to control my breathing, I spoke to Lady Lost, "Good afternoon, Lady Lost, I heard you had another call for me?" I asked before Deceitful made her exit staring in my direction.

"Oh that call long since came and left," Lady Lost replied with a smirk. "Why are you bothering me now about your endless calls anyway?" Lady Lost asked.

"I just wanted to make sure I was complying with all of your rules, of course. You said my food allowance would decrease if I didn't answer my calls. Well, every week my food allowance has been the same, and I haven't answered the calls, so I was making sure I hadn't broke one of your rules by spending my same amount every week."

After hearing my question, Deceitful rushed out of Registration like she had some important business to take care of startling the resident workers in the office. "Never mind my threat," Lady Lost said. "Sometimes things mysteriously have a way of working themselves out for everyone involved. If you will excuse me, I have a meeting beckoning me in my office," she said.

I stood there thinking, replaying what Ms. Sorrow said to me in the Old Library, the visual I had seen with Ms. Deceitful shaking hands with Lady Lost and the fact that Content reported our vouchers had not been reduced. Something is very wrong here, but what does Deceitful have to do with any of this? In the middle of my thought, Deliverance, who was seated at his desk an ear's distance away from the phone, read my confusion from the creases on my forehead. "When is the last time you spoke with your friend, Escape?" Deliverance asked while he pretended to sort through papers keeping an eye on Lady Lost's door.

"Escape is not my friend, and we haven't spoken for almost two weeks. She is more of an acquaintance," I said.

"Just because you find yourself in poverty among the rest of us poor, doesn't mean the poor can't be trusted or that we don't make good friends. We all know where you want to be and who you believe is an ideal friend. Just remember there are more rich that can't be trusted then there are poor, and from what I hear being rich can be a lonely life. Escape is your friend, a true friend that you should be glad to have and you should treat better. If you get a chance to have a friend like Escape in your whole lifetime, then you are already more rich than others," Deliverance lectured me while he sorted resident documents.

"Positive, if you don't consider anything I said to you, fine. I'm nobody anyway, but you should at least consider this: trust comes from the integrity, character, and heart of a person, not their wallet. I think you need to go visit your friend," Deliverance repeated himself about Escape being my friend before he took a break and went outside of Registration shaking his head.

So much is going on so quickly, and I'm standing here at a loss. I have been warned indirectly by two of the craziest, looniest people in this place, and they seem to believe themselves smarter than me. I can't figure out what they are saying to me. Replaying the events from this morning in my mind, we walked up to Effort Hill and saw many men from the Valley hanging around Deceitful and her children. Escape and her children were looking at us in silence and my children were waiting on me to greet Escape and make some sort of request on their behalf to play with her kids as friends.

Who is answering my calls? Who prevented Lady Lost from subtracting my food allowance? Why did Deceitful shake hands with

Lady Lost? All these unanswered questions, and I'm supposed to talk with Escape and become real friends. This is an overloaded day for my mind when No Where is supposed to be a place of no thinking.

"Momma, can we please go play with Escape's kids today?" asked Content as we stood on the edge of the Valley looking up at Escape and her children watching us.

"I don't see why we can't be friends with her kids just because you two have an inconsistent friends' relationship," Strength commented.

"Friendship, Strength."

"Huh?" asked Strength.

"Not huh, but yes, ma'am, or ma'am. I'm the mother, the boss, and it would be in the best interest of your rear end to remember that. Now, the word you need is friendship, not friends' relationship," I gave a brief English lesson on the improper use of an adjective for an abstract noun.

"Yes, ma'am, you and Ms. Escape have an inconsistent friendship," she said.

They were right, I guess. I wanted them to make friends; I just didn't want them to make friends living in poverty. And, well, Deliverance had a good argument, that a person's idea of income should not be a determinant of friendship, especially when we all have the same level of income that's equivalent to $0 in No Where.

"All right, I'll see if you can play with Escape's kids."

"Yes!" my kids cheered in unison.

I saw Praise peeking around his row of cells closer to where we stood, listening to our voices with excitement before he ran to report what we said to Harmony.

"Momma, they're walking toward us and not past us," Praise reported our movements like a sport's commentator.

There was complete silence from Praise, and we heard the sounds of the birds chirping in the trees as an audience the closer we walked to Escape. Harmony and Praise sat in front of their mother while Escape looked right, away from us, at the sky as if the sun beginning to set wanted her undivided attention and she had no idea we were coming to her cell.

"Hi, Escape," I greeted, kicking the dirt patch where grass forgot to grow.

Escape did not acknowledge my greeting. She turned her body more to the right so that I may talk to her back only. "My children were hoping to play with your kids today before inside call," I said. Praise and Harmony could not contain their urge to smile. Escape continued to ignore me like the clouds fought the sun for her undivided attention. "I don't pretend to know you, or that I even want to know you, but I do admit you have been nothing but nice to us since we arrived in No Where," I said to Escape's back. "A person willing to be nice and befriend a stranger who mistreats them is better off being a friend to themselves, so I understand if you don't want to be my friend anymore," I continued. "Does that mean our children can't be friends either?"

Praise and Harmony stood in front of their mother blocking attention to heaven's show, hoping she would answer my question. Having nowhere else to look, Escape turned to face me, squinting her eyes at me as if I was up to something else other than friendship. "Why are you really here?" she asked folding her arms across her chest, tapping her foot like she was keeping the beat of impatience.

"I have to tell you about what happened to me today and ask for any help you can give me, and offer you a sincere friendship since Deliverance has chastised me about who and what a good friend is," I replied. "Not in that order of course, friendship first, then all the rest I mentioned." It was better to be honest about everything, including the reason I was extending my friendship to her, since she clearly knew I wanted something more than just friendship but information that I could trust.

"On one condition," Escape said.

"Since when do friendships rest on conditions?" I asked.

"Since your friendship has always rested on the condition of information and what you can learn," Escape replied. This was true. She was correct. I was standing before her wanting more than her friendship, I needed information.

"Okay, what's the condition?" I urged her as time was nearing our curfew, and our children still had not played together.

"We are friends for life, no matter what, even if you manage to leave No Where, even if one of us becomes cold and stiff before the other, we are always friends for life, trusted friends. Do you accept the condition?" Escape asked still keeping the beat with her foot waiting on my answer.

"Yes, we're friends for life. We can be that, best friends, no problem. I'm sorry for mistreating you when I didn't trust you. We're trusted friends for life," I answered in full agreement.

"Great. Kids, go play, your momma and I need to talk," Escape said with an urgent low tone like there were spies in prison.

"Have you noticed Lady Lost's weird behavior lately?" Escape asked searching my eyes for an answer before my mouth did the work.

"Yes, just recently, in Registration, Deceitful was shaking hands with Lady Lost like some deal had transpired in favor of Lady Lost, and when I asked Lady Lost a question about decreasing my food allowance, she answered me pleasantly when everyone knows there is nothing pleasant about the keeper unless she gets to keep someone in the grave."

"That explains the talking walls," Escape said out loud like she arrived to an answer for a test question in class.

"What are you talking about, talking walls?" I asked. "Do you mind catching me up to your aha moment?"

"The other day, Deliverance said I missed the walls talking when I came into Registration, and now you say Lady Lost and Deceitful were shaking hands in some sort of agreement. I believe those two were the talkers on the other side of the wall from Deliverance," answered Escape.

"Earlier today, at the Old Library, Ms. Sorrow asked me who was taking my calls when I refused? Not only that, but Lady Lost never went through on her promise to reduce my food allowance for not answering my calls from Grace," I added as if I were solving a crime like Sherlock Holmes.

"Curfew, curfew call, curfew call," the officers Present and Future hollered.

"We'll talk tomorrow," I said grabbing the twins and running for our cell.

13

I fed my children toast and eggs, and their jumpers were well pressed for them to wear today. While they brushed their teeth and the twins played on the cots waiting for the second outside call, I paced the floor with thoughts about answering Grace's call and asking Deceitful about taking calls on my behalf and what Grace told her and what deal she made with Lady Lost.

"Outside call, outside call," I heard officers Future announce like an alarm that never breaks at 6 a.m.

The bolt unlocked, and Peace ran downstairs for the door. "Why are you so excited about today?" I questioned Peace as he grabbed the knob and turned around with this look of agony on his face like I gave him a timed calculus question to answer.

"Momma, we have friends again," Peace said. "I'll wait on the step for you to come out with the twins. I'm excited to play with other kids and not have the worry of your approval of them lingering in our atmosphere. Make the twins hurry, don't forget you have three minutes before the bolt locks again, and we have never seen what happens if you remain inside after the Outside call," Peace said as if saying he would be innocent if we get caught inside due to our failed timeliness.

"Don't you worry, Peace, we'll make it outside," I said taking the knot out of Truth's shoe and listening to my girls' anxiousness in their voices to join Peace outside.

"Strength, grab the twins, I'll get the lunch," Content instructed.

"Momma, did you take your medicine last night?" Strength asked.

"Yes, I took my medicine, and it's time to complete another medical form for more injections to be sent to Registration today, don't forget to remind me," I said to Strength stepping out of our cell and closing the door just before the lock bolted.

I looked up from the door knob directly into an officer Future's eyes standing in the grass patch next to the step from the door. "That was a close one," he said before commanding the rest of the officers to return to their street post.

"Positive, come with me. Kids, play up here in front of Positive's door where we can see you from over there," Escape ordered pointing toward the cells where Deceitful lived.

"Where are we going?" I asked rhetorically in an effort to keep some type of conversation going to distract me from the nerves in my stomach of what today might hold.

"Just follow where I lead and act like you know what I'm talking about," mumbled Escape, speed walking to almost a run to Deceitful's cell.

"Good morning," Escape said, pushing Deceitful against the tin wall of her cell before she could turn and exit her step good.

"It's not going to be a good anything for you if you put your hands on me again. What do you want?" asked Deceitful, ready to move around after we blocked her into the cell.

"I want you to tell my friend, Positive, what deal you made with Lady Lost in exchange for your increased food allowance, or you're right it will not be a good morning for any of us," answered Escape, pushing Deceitful backwards hitting her head against the door.

All of the residents in the Present area noticed we were ganging up on Deceitful, and no one came to her defense. Effort Hill just gathered closely like they were playing with their children in order to hear our conversation clearly.

"I didn't make no deals with Lady Lost," Deceitful lied hoping her elevated voice would send her some help from the men in the Valley she had been sharing her food allowance with, but no one came to her aid because no one likes a snitch.

"Why are you looking around for help? No one is going to help or save you from me," Escape said shoving Deceitful a second time while I went to find a big stick to pick up and swing slowly back and forth. "See there is a difference between you and I," Escape began to enlighten Deceitful with me standing there trying to look meaner than Escape like I was going to bash Deceitful' s head in any moment, even though I've never had to hit anyone before in my life. "The difference between you and I, is that I was born here in No Where. I didn't choose No Where, it chose me, unlike your obvious choice to come here because you failed at manipulating your way through the pockets of rich men. You are not like any of us here, not even like the prostitutes my daddy pimped because they didn't enjoy the way they chose to survive, and you look forward to it," Escaped said in a harsh whispered tone to the left of Deceitful's ear.

"The only thing no one told you is when you signed up to be in No Where, that was a permanent move for people like you. There is no getting out for you because there is no one here you can manipulate," she continued. "See I have a choice to try America if I want," Escape continued to teach Deceitful the rules of No Where that were never shared with me. "Every seasoned person here knows me and would never turn on me, but a fresh Haitian woman like yourself could never gain the loyalty that I have within the short amount of time you've been here. So I'll do you a favor, tell me what we want to know, and I'll let you go without the Valley having to make a trip up here to bother you and your kids a bit."

"How did you know I was Haitian?" Deceitful asked interested only for the sake of her vanity.

"Your chocolate skin and your French accent gave you away mixed with my lucky guess. I haven't lived my entire life with a pimp as a father to not know the difference between accents of one low-class prostitute from a high-class prostitute. I pay attention to all the different kinds of people that find themselves here for one reason or another," Escape paused in her memory abruptly. "Stop changing the subject, and answer my question, or my new friend here knows just where to put a stick that would give you splinters for months," she said angrily.

"Okay, okay, it's no loss to me, I have to watch my weight, and the quality of this food is not a good bargaining tool, so I'll tell you what you want to know," she said annoyed by Escape's hand pinning her to the dirty townhome. "I answered the phone once when Positive refused to answer her calls from her attorney. Lady Lost caught me answering the call and made a deal with me to continue to answer the calls in exchange for food allowance increase every month. Lady Lost said what you just said, no one leaves from No Where, like she had the support of the government to keep us here until we all become—"

"Cold and stiff," Escape and I joined in on Lady Lost's favorite repetitive words as Deceitful concluded her confession.

"So, why did you do it if you didn't really care about the food?" I asked still gripping the stick.

"I thought your attorney would have some information about how to get out of here, but he kept rambling on about writing a letter to a parole board or something and the way to write the letter. Well, none of that helps me because I haven't been indicted yet, and I don't plan to be here long enough to get indicted."

Deceitful continued, "I was just buying time for me to return to America before Supercilious trapped me here. Lady Lost said if I answered the calls, she would convince Supercilious to prosecute someone else as there are many people living below poverty in America, which bought me more free time. Can I go now?" Deceitful asked Escape while I turned away from them with a headache from holding a frown that was supposed to cause Deceitful to fear us more.

14

Staring at Deceitful like she had better protect herself and children from danger from now on, Escape released her to the morning removing her hand from Deceitful's chest at the same time the intercom squeaked with a loud noise before we heard Lady Lost.

"Attention, attention to all my residents, Ms. Sorrow was found cold and still in her townhome this morning, and I am preparing to be compensated after her cremation. If there is anyone who knew Ms. Sorrow who would like to see her one last time, report to Registration immediately before officers Past place her into the hearse and escort her body to a fiery resting place," then the intercom went silent.

My lungs sank into my feet as weights preventing me from walking and causing me to gasp for air that took too long to reach every bronchus after hearing Lady Lost's announcement. Finally, taking her gaze off of Deceitful walking toward the Valley, Escape caught me in time before I fell to the ground. "Are you okay? I know you just heard that crazy old lady Ms. Sorrow died, but you started to not look so good, and I thought your mysterious illness maybe giving you problems," Escape continued to ramble before I interrupted her.

"Ms. Sorrow was not crazy, she was not crazy," I protested. "She had a family, and she helped me, she made me want to fight again," I cried, determined to walk down to the Valley in spite of the sick feeling in the pit of my stomach and my disbelief that she was gone.

Escape followed behind me after waving up the hill for our children to join us, then she pointed two fingers at Deceitful to threaten that she was watching her and her kids. When we reached the end of Valley Street, there were many residents standing on the sidewalk bidding there farewells to Ms. Sorrow. Some were crying and others mumbling to Ms. Sorrow, while Lady Lost looked impatiently at the mourners who surrounded the hearse. Approaching the hearse, I found Ms. Sorrow sleeping on her back in her white jumper with her hands interlocked and resting on her stomach. Looking at her infuriated me. "Where are her T-shirts she had tied around her leg, where are her garbage bags, and where is the bowl she balanced on her head?" I screamed at the residents and Lady Lost. "She is not leaving here without her stuff," I said running around to the driver and snatching the keys out of the ignition storming in the direction of her cell.

"I understand, someone close to you has passed, but we need to finish our business of ridding ourselves of the body, so give the keys back to the driver now," demanded Lady Lost as she followed me with officers Past.

"I'm not giving the keys to anyone until all of Ms. Sorrow's stuff is placed in her casket with her, so if you want to make your money off her quickly, then someone had better get her belongings quickly out of this cell!" I yelled with tears streaming down my face.

"What difference does it make? She can't take those stupid T-shirts, trash bag, and bowl with her wherever she's going, so why does it matter if it's in the casket or not?" Lady Lost asked motioning to officers Past to unlock Ms. Sorrow's cell. "I think the clean white jumper is suitable for a proper burning of the dead," she said standing outside.

"I'm getting her stuff or no keys," I hollered putting the keys into my yellow jumper hiding them inside my bra. Turning on the light in Ms. Sorrow's cell made my soul laugh and my spirit cry. Her walls were filled with pictures of her family that dated back to the beginning of her marriage to Love. There were pictures of Happy asleep at the dinner table, pictures of Henrietta and Hope playing with their dolls in the bedroom of their old house. One picture had captured her Henry dressed in Love's factory clothes pretending to work and provide for the family.

I went upstairs in search of her stuff and found drawings along the wall of her memories with her family, and everyone was laughing, full of joy. I searched in her room where there was a shrine on every wall of her Love that she had drawn capturing the hugs he had given her. I could feel his soul connected to hers as my fingers went over his eyes that stared into her eyes as they held hands in bed. Ms. Sorrow was sane and with her family every day. We were the crazy ones, I thought, finding her stuff in the bathroom.

Marching down the stairs and giving her stuff to two residents who assured me they would put the items on Ms. Sorrow, I brushed past Lady Lost almost knocking her down as I returned to the hearse keeping the key. "Thank you," I said to the residents, then turning to Ms. Sorrow, I correctly maneuvered the trash bag and t-shirts along her knees and placed the bowl across her chest before bidding her my farewell.

Tapping the casket twice, I spoke to Ms. Sorrow, "Tell Mr. Love I said hello, and tell Happy to stop playing so much if he's there. If your kids haven't made it to you because they are still alive here, then watch over them like you always wanted to because there's no one to keep you separated from them anymore. And don't worry about me, these tears are from joy only." I cried tapping the casket again before handing the keys to Lady Lost and walking away toward my future and leaving Ms. Sorrow in my past.

Many residents from the Valley looked as Escape and I walked shoulder to shoulder like friends toward Effort Hill with our kids trailing behind us. I could not stop the stream of tears that flooded the neckline of my jumper like a river. Escape remained silent walking alongside me until we reached her cell.

"I never really knew crazy old Sorrow," she said with a smirk trying to cheer me up.

"I'm not sad, I only cry from tears of joy," I told myself remembering Ms. Sorrow's words to me. "She wasn't crazy, she was never crazy."

"Okay, old Sorrow wasn't crazy," Escape agreed, "Do you want to continue with our plan to get you out of here?" asked Escape quietly as to not seem disrespectful to the deceased.

"What plan? There was no plan. Grace wants me to write a begging letter to the parole board as if I haven't begged enough in this lifetime."

"Like I said, a plan, so do you want to work on it?" Escape asked a second time. "I hear work can be a distraction from grief."

"No, not today, I want my Content to order my injections and retrieve one from the refrigerator in Registration. I want to sit in front of my cell watching the last sunset on Ms. Sorrow and never forget her or her family," I said in tears leaving Escape's cell.

"Okay, then tomorrow, we'll work on it tomorrow." Escape yelled, "Positive you have a lot of heart, more heart than most people I know! As a person with heart, you have to remember everyone loses people, money, and their dreams in life at some point, but a loss isn't forever. When people become cold and stiff, you will rejoin them on the other side in the warmth of their love. When you lose a mate, they either return with goodness for you, or they return to show you your goodness without them. When money leaves, it always returns, my dad used to say, and dreams become your reality when you believe they are more than a dream. When you remember this in your heart, everything will be restored and you will heal," she said. "So tomorrow we're working on a plan." Pleased with the idea, she smiled and waved in search for my agreement.

"Tomorrow will take care of itself," I replied to Escape without taking my eyes off the sunset. *Did she really give me a lecture I received with no argument? Wow, unbelievable*, I thought.

15

"What do you think I'm supposed to write in this letter to the parole board that they don't already know from researching my trial?" I asked Grace on the phone while Lady Lost was eavesdropping and Deliverance was smiling pretending not to overhear my conversation with my attorney.

"You should write a letter of truth that makes them see you and know you as a person and not as a statistic in America's economic equation. Write a letter about determination, self-will, about poverty in America," Grace suggested.

"I will do my best, and I'll let you know when I have mailed it, okay?" I said.

"You have two weeks to submit this letter considering October 31 is tomorrow," Grace informed me.

"Were you Ms. Sorrow's attorney?" I asked Grace, waiting on the truth or a lie. I don't know who I can trust anymore since I've been exiled to No Where at the will of a faceless, cultureless, powerful atomic idea called America. There is always the possibility that he was annoying me with this letter just to make himself feel better about my verdict.

"Yes, I was Ms. Sorrow's attorney. I know our friend has recently passed away in her sleep this year. I knew Ms. Sorrow, and she knew about you and your family before you arrived to No Where. Ms. Sorrow had brain cancer, and she wore a bowl on her head awaiting her new brain to come from heaven so she could one day find her children. After telling her about this good feeling I had about you, she told me she would look after you and your five kids because you reminded her of a fight she had long lost the energy to battle when she saw you your first night there. That's why Ms. Sorrow was always there when you needed her only because she said strong people need to have their strength and can't be worn down by the sad details of another's complaints and doubts if they were going to survive in the battle of their minds against poverty."

I held the phone close to my ear and closed my eyes imagining Ms. Sorrow was speaking to me before she would tap the table while Grace continued, "Ms. Sorrow was very fond of you, and she believed that you had only lost the first round in your fight against poverty and that you had many winning fights left in you for your family and others when you returned to America.

"Ms. Sorrow would not permit me to share this with you until she found herself in her husband's arms again. She said she knew you wouldn't let her rest until you had more details about her because you're too nosey for all the facts of people you meet in this life's journey. Just like a good fighter studies their opponents before battle, you study people before standing with them or against them in any battle. Yes, I knew our friend very well!"

"Ms. Sorrow mentioned you were her attorney in one of our conversations at the Old Library. I never asked her about your relationship with her, and she never volunteered the information." I added, "It was a test question to make certain you were honestly helping me and not making yourself feel better about the verdict."

"Fine, Positive, now you know I've been honest with you through this entire journey. Now, will you please get the letter written on time?" Grace asked. "Just write and submit the letter, don't worry about the rest."

"I will write the letter," I agreed before hanging up the phone.

I heard Lady Lost hang up the phone, and I turned toward Deliverance, thanking him for watching my kids in front of Registration's door.

"Ms. Fighter, it was no problem to watch your kids, you know I love a good war," he said to me laughing and then looking at the frus-

118

trated face of Lady Lost because she knew she had just lost another family when the choses return to America.

Lady Lost walked to the door shouting at me. "You should know that your food allowance has been suspended, and I will have the officers remove any food you have remaining in your townhome that I gave you!

"Deliverance, tell the officers Present to bring Deceitful to my office now!" she continued to yell as the door closed.

I exited Registration right into the arms of my twins and laughs of my older children as they watched Praise and Harmony show them some dance they learned from Escape. Today is a beautiful day. "What do we do first?" asked Escape.

"Write and rewrite a letter to the parole board until it's ready to be mailed," I answered. "Oh, you heard Lady Lost, we have no food any longer, so I'll be weak over the next several days, but I will write the letter," I assured my children and Escape walking to the Old Library.

16

Every day for the past week I wrote and rewrote my letter to the parole board. My children and I lost a lot of weight, and Escape couldn't spare anymore food for us. The twins cried at night from hunger pains, and my older children argued upstairs trying to remain respectful to me when they came downstairs watching me write. I became obsessed digesting every word for nourishment night and day.

"Outside call, outside call," officers Future announced. My children rushed to help me get dressed, and we went outside to a feast laid on the ground before our door. There were apples and oranges, cans of beans, bread, and water. Deliverance, Escape, and a few other residents stood there smiling with tears of joy. Peace beat everyone to the ground, biting into an apple in his right hand and holding a piece of bread in his left. He had no questions about anything for anyone for the first time in his life.

The twins jumped up and down with excitement while Strength gave them an orange. Content thanked everyone for the food, holding the can of beans with a tight grip, making sure no one had changed their minds about their gift of food.

I grabbed an apple to eat, but I preferred to continue digesting my letter. On our way to the Old Library we saw Ms. Deceitful and her children dressed in white jumpers with the letters "V-S-P" written on their backs. "Momma, what do the letters stand for on Miss Deceitful's back?" Peace asked chewing a piece of orange.

"It doesn't matter, it's not on our backs. We have a letter to finish and mail," I said with enthusiasm changing the subject. I had fun walking to the Old Library watching our kids chase each other and Escape talk my ear off about the bright sunny day and prison gossip of newcomers.

Dear Parole Board,

My name is Positively Chose. My family and I were drafted to No Where because we don't economically exist in America according to the new law. My family was subjected to this prison because we have no money and the American government refuses to feed us or supply our medical benefits any longer. My family's credentials align with America's three rules that are required for citizenship: 1) A native of American soil, 2) obtain a higher education, 3) be self-disciplined to work hard.

Those rules are imprinted into the minds and hearts of my family for generations, and yet I was found guilty of poverty. Before we were deported here, during my trial I painfully heard repeatedly from several individuals in charge of the employment sector that my education made me overqualified for the work they had available. My credit score was too low to be an approved job applicant, and my zip code rested in the wrong areas of the city, therefore all of my efforts for upward mobility were rejected. These employers in court were poverty's accomplices to my life sentence.

I was diagnosed with multiple sclerosis, an affliction of my brain, but not an affliction of my thinking and willpower to succeed.

America convicted me of poverty with no association to laziness or lack of education because I am educated or too motivated to be lazy. I was guilty of poverty, plain and simple. Poverty is the state of poor people's wallet parallel to the wallets of a few rich individuals in this country, and I was guilty of having the poor people's empty wallet.

Over the past year of living in prison, the inmates have taught me that poverty has no respect for culture, race, family, education, or prior wealth of a person—it is poverty. From listening to the inmates here, I understand that the opposite of poverty is wealth at the cost of lies, war, and prostitution of one's character and integrity until they become an enemy of peace for a dollar. An enemy of peace is too high a price to pay for any American citizen. I refuse to be an enemy of myself in an attempt to escape poverty.

My explanation for my poverty condition is not to persuade you to release me on the idea that I will not remain poor for the duration of my time on earth, but to enlighten you on the fact that poverty is not the fault of one aspect of the American people whether they have had a teenage pregnancy, or are a neglected veteran, uneducated, or an illegal immigrant, it's simply suffering people who need help..

Poverty is no more crime worthy than the questionable gains of one's wealth. My suffering through poverty does not make me a criminal of America.

* * *

Escape and her family, along with my family, all walked across the street to the mailbox underneath the light pole and mailed our last opportunity to be free. We waited in the Valley for Grace to call while watching the kids chase each other up and down the sidewalk. "Positive, you have a phone call, Positive, there is a call for you in Registration," Lady Lost reported over the intercom.

"Hello."

"Hi, Positive, is that you?" Grace asked.

"Yes, it's me."

"Did you write the letter?"

"Yes, I wrote the letter and mailed it," I answered.

"Good, that's good!" said Grace.

"Yes, it is, it is a good day," I said, hanging up the phone.

ABOUT THE AUTHOR

Rachel Leonard was born as an identical twin in Champaign-Urbana, Illinois in 1982. She graduated from Donnelly College in Kansas City, Kansas in 2009 with four children under the age of ten. In love with writing and English, Rachel continued her education as a Bloch Scholar at the University of Missouri-Kansas City where she graduated in 2011. Recently, she had her fifth child in 2014. Now currently working as an accounting clerk, Rachel writes daily in her journal and takes notes on everything around her in anticipation of writing her second book. Motivated and determined, she plans on one day being a legendary writer.

CPSIA information can be obtained at www.ICGtesting.com
Printed in the USA
BVOW08s0204301115

428778BV00001B/53/P